No Time

The First Hour

R. Jean Mathieu

No Time: The First Hour

R. Jean Mathieu

First printing July 2014.
7 6 5 4 3 2 1 0 9 8

Table of Contents

Dedication

Dedicated to Sara Garcia, Lachlan Atcliffe, Brandi Bennett, Mark Couch, Alexia Jasmene, and especially to Diana Hsu.

Acknowledgements

This book would not exist without the excellent copy-editing skills of Jenna Barker, nor would it look so lovely without the design skills of Torie Gervais. I am indebted also to Torie for giving me the impetus to actually *start* this book, to the men and women of #fleet for standing by me all these years whether I'm writing or not, and to Dean Wesley Smith for getting me to start writing again at all.

I would also like to thank Mrs. Talka, for teaching me to read, Ray Bradbury, for teaching me to write, and Jack London, for teaching me how to sell what I write. Thank you to Aetherco and to Audrey Niffenegger for opening my mind to the possibilities of time travel. *Gracias* to Nancy Uznanski, for cursing quite freely in Spanish for my benefit. And, of course, the thank yous to Mother and Father, for making it all possible on a long-ago moonlit chessboard.

I

April 18, 2014 – 5:55:32 AM

I'm in bed when the call comes in. Time-actives, we have a lot of very clever ways to talk to one another, but most of the time the simple way is best.

It takes me awhile to come together, all lead-limbed and tired like I am. My wife murmurs, turns over, tries to throw her strapping arm over me. Hold me close. I want her to. I have done a man's job and I want a man's rest with Rachel's arms around me, her warmth at my back, her burnished bronze hair falling over my neck and shoulder. But the phone could be anyone: Will to tell me that my bail-skip is gone again and so I won't collect, some young woman in trouble, some husband wanting to find his missing wife, a suicide, a runaway son…and I am a detective. It is my job to answer when I would rather sleep.

"Gabriel…" Rachel whines, as I slip out of the bed. I think that is what she says. Her face is up against the pillow.

The fog outside is cold, and makes the whole house chilly in the dark. It helps to wake me up. I lurch to the dresser at the foot of the bed, where I left my cell charging. My hands fumble over the case when I try to open it. Older model, flip phone, does not look suspicious if I'm at work in 1995.

"*¿Hola?*" I mutter, voice thick with unfinished sleep, as I stagger down the stairs and into the hall. "What time is it?"

I stop, and stagger in the other direction. Debbie-Anne, Rachel's sister, is sleeping in the guest bedroom.

"Gooch." It's Will. "There's something you need to see. I'll be there in ten minutes."

"Will, is it here?" I ask. Of course not, Will does not call California's only time-active detective in the middle of the night on mundane business.

"No, I'll take you there," he says.

"That's good, because I haven't slept." I tell him. To skip, you need a clear head and plenty of rest. I skipped once while drunk, and twice without a good night's sleep. The second time, I came out the right time…but twenty miles above the surface of the Atlantic Ocean. I do not want to repeat the trick.

Yesterday, my yesterday, I snatched a bail-skip in 2017 and brought him to the mundane authorities for his parole hearing in 2012…but not before turning him over to the Time Cops first. They make certain that when he is expected to appear in court, he is there. And if he is sent to jail, he will not be able to just snap his fingers and escape.

I needed to keep going for almost twenty-four hours, my time. Most bail-skips, even the time-actives, they only change their time and place. They do not change their work, their hobbies, their habits. This *hijo de chingada madre* is a little more clever than most, he changed his name and his profession, both among us and in the everyday world. But he did not change his favorite meal, a kind of Japanese soup his mother used to make. I had a good tip that he went to Kutsenmoto's just after coming to 2017, so I staked it out all day. I drank coffee after coffee and felt my ass start to go from sitting so much. He came along with me, but only after I made it clear he could not skip away. Time-skipping in a restaurant full of witnesses would land him in worse trouble than he already was. I also let him finish his soup.

Lots of skipping, lots of tension, lots of waiting. It makes a man tired. I came home around eleven, to my wife Rachel cleaning up the remains of a potluck. Her sister, Debbie-Anne, is visiting us from Texas. They were like night and day: Debbie-Anne is small, round, and soft, from the blonde curls of their mother to the cowboy boots she wears over her blue jeans. Rachel towers over her (and me), her coppery hair cinched back in a ponytail, wearing a rainbow scarf, the sweater that Debbie-Anne knit last Christmas, and a flowery skirt that swished at her ankles. When I came in, Debbie-Anne was mock-complaining that Rachel had cost her a date.

"I only threatened him a little." Rachel replied, in the same tone. They stuck their tongues out at each other, like schoolgirls.

I'd have enjoyed their company, especially Rachel's, rather than gone skipping off to 2017. But my wife was not happy that I was home so late, and I am not happy to be woken up early.

"See you in ten." Will repeats.

I go to the study, my home office, my man's place. I don't feel like torturing my eyes with the light yet, but then, I do not need it. I know the room and I know what I'm looking for. In the closet, there is a spare change of clothes — *es bueno,* being prepared. I work my way into the jeans and the button down, which make me look like any other Mexican in California who does not have to work with his hands. They feel comfortable, lived-in. Small favors.

In the third, 'stuck' drawer of my desk, I keep my up-and-down box. If things follow you through time, they might not *que será, será* as well as you. If there are two copies of my notebook, my Swiss Army knife, or the binoculars, I know I must take the copy at the back. I must take it because it is *mas joven*, younger, and I do not break the Twelve Laws of Time.

There are four guns there, two in each section.

"*Ay yai yai*," I whisper, "I am a busy man."

I pack the *mas joven* set: The Colt Python in its shoulder holster, and the 2-inch .38 Detective Special at my ankle. The familiar weight makes me feel more together, something I need right now. People think I'm sentimental for carrying revolvers, and this is fine. If I pull the Colt in 1943, I do not have to answer to the Time Police, as I would if I pull a Desert Eagle. Also, .38 and .357 bullets are always cheap. I like that.

After filling my pockets and holsters, I slip into my chukka boots and throw on an old, light leather coat, both to cover the Python and keep out the chill. Will's knock comes a few minutes later, while I'm standing at the coffee pot, my stomach gurgling for the hot, black, bitter brew. *Chingao.* I switch it off, take a deep breath, and go to the door to let the chill in.

Det. Sgt. William Howe of the Time Police is a middle-aged *gringo*, sandy hair going grey, with green eyes. He's ageless, well-built, nice full smile, practices his skipping every day…everything a proper time-active should be. A few more years of this, who knows? Rank nine or ten, maybe, and meet the Legion who will inherit the Earth. In a decade or two, he might even join the Legion. I hope he gets it. He's an *hombre de verdad*. He's pulled my fat from the fire many times.

He does not look so good this morning. He trembles a little, and the full mouth keeps turning down. He looks at me with wide eyes, like he cannot believe that he found me, Gabriel, at The Home of Gabriel Caballero y Gutiérrez and Rachel McCoy-Caballero (Rachel made the sign herself...*¿las mujeres, verdad?*).

"Will, you look like shit." I greet him with a smirk.

There's an awkward little pause, then Will clears his throat.

"Not as much as you do, Gooch."

"I hope you pulled me from my warm bed, with my warm wife in it, for a good reason." I narrow my bloodshot eyes at him threateningly. "And I hope you brought coffee."

Will shakes his head.

"No time," he says, "I...look, Gooch, just come out here. I can't...you have to see for yourself."

Now I am worried, and all the sleep disappears. Not the tired, no, but the sleep, yes. Will could have just gone to get coffee, then come back with it. If he can't...maybe there is no time, as he says. Maybe we are going into a nexus, and such frivolous trips are too dangerous.

And he is acting frightened. A full Detective Sergeant of the Temporal Security Bureau, who's investigated grisly and unnatural things from 1849 to the red line in 2112, is frightened. This man, I have seen him three steps from reality, hunted, beaten, fighting to breathe, find the Free Will anarchists responsible and use them to resync before leading the posse himself to rub them out. I have seen him quietly accept the untimely death of his own mother, *que será, será*, and the loss of his partner in the fires of 9/11, ensuring all those deaths happen correctly. I have worked with him to clean every trace of corpses out of time, including that one case where she was spread over most of an acre.

This man is *frightened*.

I step out into the porch, which blinks the light on automatically. Will must have skipped in, and not disturbed the light…but then why not skip out…?

He throws his arm around me, and takes a deep breath. As one, we blink.

The first thing I hear is the cry of a lonesome gull. Damn flying rats.

And when I open my eyes, I can see the chill fog, an all-encompassing blanket of grey. It is as cold as it was at my house, a wet chill that rattles your ribs. Later in the day, it will be nice and sunny and perfect beach temperature, but now it's chilly and damp as the mistral. I need to close my eyes a few more times because even with the fog cover it is too bright for me, and I can feel the stabbing pain in my eyes.

I look around, and get my bearings. With a lungful of air, I can smell the early-morning salt tang of the back bay, the rotting seaweed and the clear clean scent of the fog. We are standing on the short strand of beach where Rachel likes to come clamming some mornings. Just up the bay from the Natural History Museum, but before the eucalyptus trees crowd up to the shore. Behind me is the county road that turns into Main Street at Morro Bay city lines…and at this time of morning, thankfully deserted.

"What time is it?" I ask.

"April 20, at 6:45 in the morning," he replies. He has enough pull to have time-tellers installed in his brain. I only have the basics inside my skull. I know that I've skipped two days, zero hours, thirty-nine minutes, and twenty seconds…but I foolishly did not check the clock when we left.

"Easter Sunday." I note. Will nods once. "We should be at Mass."

He doesn't reply. There is a long silence I can feel in my gut.

"So what do I need to see?" I ask.

At first, I think it is a log, or a piece of driftwood. But no, as we walk closer, I see it is a body. We are alone on the beach, and I feel the loneliness like the morning chill. And I feel something turn in my empty guts when we get close enough.

I know those shoulders. Those short, muscular legs, pride of the SLO Running Club. That curly black goat's-hair. The leather jacket, identical to the one I'm wearing.

Even face down, I recognize my own dead body.

I mutter an oath to Mary, full of Grace, and cover my mouth. Will stands by, breathing quick and shallow, and points me up the beach. I go and look at the bark of a eucalyptus for a few minutes. My whole body is shaking, and my stomach feels both empty and full of cement at once. It's one thing to see a dead body, to move it, to clean up after it…it's something different when it is your own.

I can feel livor mortis forming in my feet. *Chingao*, I'm a private detective! Murders are for the police! Even if I am time-active, I do not want to get involved with this. Death and divorce are both nasty enough most PIs stay away from them. But this is one death I can't get away from, can I...?

Will lays a hand on my shoulder. I turn to him, carefully not far enough to see the ...thing that I can't stop thinking about. With his other hand, he offers a cigarette. Automatically, I push it away. Not since the marriage. Rachel and I are a healthy people.

My brain latches on the thing that I cannot look at.

...maybe not so healthy.

"This is for the police," I say. "Murder is not a PI's jurisdiction. Murder of one of us least of all."

"You're the best man to find the bastard," Will replies. "And you know we'll get him. I'll round up the posse myself. Besides...this gives you a chance to know something about the murder before it happens."

And murder it must be. Anything that does not kill me has already been prevented...Disease? I laugh at disease. Gunshot? I already had Kevlar. Poison? I ate the antidote already. Old age? I must ask politely and file the papers, but I can stave off old age a very long time. We are a healthy people, because we know it is coming.

No one can kill a time-active...except another time-active. I have heard that often enough at the café.

Now I am starting to think. How was it done? And why?

I take a deep breath and mentally divorce myself from the reality. For now. Later, while I am driving around town, I'll shake. Fuck the coffee, I could use a shot of tequila. Or a bottle. Yes, a bottle of *reposado* tequila with Rachel, salt, lemon wedges, going shot for shot…that would be nice.

Will is standing by, fidgeting. He keeps glancing at the tree. It is cold. And I need to find out what happened to …to the body.

"We're here before the police." I say, still looking at the tree. Inch by inch, I turn. I take in the bay. It is grey with fog, a shade lighter now. "I assume the police will not find it?"

Will shakes his head.

"This is a job for us." Will says. One of our *amigos*, Matthew Park, is a member of the Morro Bay Police Department. But that is not what Will means. Will means the Time Cops…and the Eternist community as a whole. No one kills one of us with impunity.

"How did you know?"

"Anonymous tipoff," he says, lighting his cigarette, "left on my porch with a knock. Could've been any one of us."

The flick of his lighter is a spark in the peculiar gloom of a foggy dawn. I nod.

"Have you called Park?" I ask.

He shakes his head, and repeats the words: "*Que será, será.*"

What will be, will be. First of the Twelve Laws of Time. The Twin Towers are always falling, somewhen. Francesca always marries that asshole, somewhen. I always save Rachel and Debbie-Anne McCoy, somewhen. I always die on this strand of beach, somewhen. Moments, frozen in time, things you can't change…no matter how much you want to. It would destroy everything.

Park will show, and probably Morgan too, because they are known to be here. I will probably call them. But not until I am ready for them to come.

"How long ago?" I ask him.

"Almost real-time," he says. "He woke me up in the middle of the night."

His eyes go slack while he consults his internal clock-bugs.

"4:22:03 AM. Friday morning, of course."

"When'd you get here?"

"6:36 this morning."

I let my gaze slide, finally from the lapping water of the bay to the mound on the beach. The body. My ...the body.

I have run until my legs were on fire, run so hard that when I climbed on the bicycle I could only fall off, because my legs were so tired. But those were glorious, alive days, when my body thrummed with animal vitality, my skin sliding with sweat, my throat laughing and hoarse, my wife as overheated and loud and alive next to me. But this, this is a march of the dead. I have never taken thirteen steps as hard as the steps I take towards the body that morning.

Clothing – leather jacket. I finger mine. Jeans. Hiking boots, leather. Athletic socks.

"Will?" I ask. Will is running his hands up the bark of the tree, contemplative, but I do not know why. "You are certain the police will not find..."

I choke. Only a little.

"...him?"

Will nods, strides up to me. "I'll help you flip him over."

I take the body in hand and turn him over, a prayer escaping my lips as I do. I have not prayed much since the 30s. He is stiff, but mostly in the small joints…the wrists and hands, and in the face. Rigor mortis, not too far along…three to six hours maybe?

The face is mottly grey, all the earthy color that Rachel loves so much all drained out.

Rachel… *Madre de Diós, me Rachel…*

Has she already got the phone call, the ghost that keeps her awake? Does she already know she's…

I shake it off. Not now. I will go to Happy Jacks ten years ago and drink for hours and sleep it off if I need it, but *not. Now.*

I take one of the hands. It is an eerie feeling, but preferable to thinking about widowhood. The backs of the hands are angry purple, the palms dead grey. There are abrasions at the knuckles, skin torn off wounds that will never heal. Defense wounds. I lift up the knit sweater Rachel's sister made me. The belly is just as grey as the palms, but start running to violet and a deep, florid wine color at the sides.

"He died on his back." I note. "Not long ago."

Will checks his watch.

"Between two and four." He says. I nod. We meet eyes.

The cause of death is clear enough…purplish bands of bruising at the neck. I would bet good money the carotid artery's been compressed, probably with the thyroid and hyroid cartilage crushed in the bargain. The bruises are even, and there aren't any telltale crescent marks. So, strangled, but ligature strangulation. I don't see any rope burns or patterns, just some lateral lines where the skin was pinched. Cloth?

What kind of cloth?

I shove back the leather jacket's sleeve, and the sweater underneath it. Bruises, some lost in the purpling of the livor mortis, all along the underside of the forearm. Some of them are bright livid violet, in the blanched flesh where the dead arm was off the ground. At least the poor bastard didn't go down easy. Still, it's one dead Mexican on the beach and no murderer in sight.

I flip open the leather jacket. One of the pockets is ripped open, cut from inside. Holster's in place. Empty. Will holds the left leg up while I shove the pant-leg along the beefy calf. Ankle-holster's empty, too. Did he at least get a shot off? Is the murderer's blood some-where on the beach?

That's my last thought when the flashes come.

Park and Morgan announce themselves with polite little flashes, down behind the rocks near the Natural History Museum. Out of the mist, they calmly emerge. Officer Matt Park looks younger than me, all baby-faced, but he's really in his mid-30s, wiry, with long arms and legs and twinkling brown eyes. At one hip, for all the world to see, he's got his service S&W .38. Just as I am a detective, both to time travelers and to everyone else, he is all cop.

Sean Morgan, Esq., has cheekbones like you'd cut out of a tree and eyes the color of the fog. As always, he's carrying his soft leather "Bill and Ted" bag. Morgan is fuller at the waist and shoulder than Park, but do not be fooled. He is first to volunteer when the posse is called, and handles himself well, despite taking seriously all the little laws of time the rest of us honor with our hypocrisy. I would make a joke about lawyers and bloodthirst, but I am a little rattled at the moment.

"Where have you come from?" I ask.

"Yesterday." Morgan says, passing me a white baggie. "You asked me to bring these. Good morning, Gooch."

Yesterday...so we may be coming to a nexus after all. A nexus where I die. A couple of different kinds of no time.

"Sorry," Park adds, smirking, "they're a day old."

Morgan gives him a withering glare while I open it. A bagel from Top Dog, with cream cheese, and a black coffee. I sniff. 2Dogs' Arabica blend...and fresh, the bagel is still piping hot.

They brought my favorite coffee. My stomach declares that I am not rattled enough to turn away good food like this.

"*Gracias,*" I say.

"You're welcome," Morgan replies, his gaze sliding to the body. I take a long sip of the coffee and nearly scald my tongue. It reminds me that I am still alive...for now.

Park looks out over the beach, too, and all the good humor falls away from his face like grime in the shower.

"Will!" He calls. "What are you doing there?"

"Looking over the body." He says, straightening up. He looks pale. Park rolls his eyes.

"And tearing up the sand." Park notes, his Officer Park mask sliding into place. All the youth is gone out of his face. He is no longer a boyish joker. He is all business and it's exactly what I need right now. "I'm not putting up the tape, but Jesus Christ, just ...stand where you are while we scope the scene out."

I look down in the sand. *Madre de Diós*, I'm foolish today. This is a rank one mistake, and I feel my gut fall and my face flush. Between us, Will and I have torn up the sand all around the body and across the beach, wiping out any good footprints or other evidence. I can almost hear the voice of my old mentor, back in the 1500s, biting my ear off for disturbing the crime scene.

"Where'd you guys go?" Park demands. Will and I quickly review our movements since our arrival.

"Gooch, you're with me," he says, "Morgan, you half as good at figuring out time-active deaths as you are at causing them?"

Morgan just gives Park another flinty look. I bite into my bagel. It is steamy and warm and tangy and deliciously life-affirming.

"Okay, guys, keep clear of the body and for God's sake, don't step on anyone's footprints." He tries to mimic one of Morgan's flinty looks, addressed to Will and me. "At least, any more than you already have. Gooch here has an excuse. After this, Detective Howe, I'd *love* to hear yours."

"Look here, kid..."

"Don't you 'kid' me." Another Officer Park calmly arrives, flashing in behind Will and laying two hands on his shoulders. "This is a fucking crime scene. You know better than to dance all over it."

"This is a time-active crime scene," Will spins on his heel and growls, "and I outrank you, *Officer*, in the relevant jurisdiction."

"When you two are finished, we could use your help." Morgan notes drolly, examining the print my chukkas left in front of the eucalyptus. "If you want, I can sort the jurisdictional issues for you for my usual retainer and fee schedule."

The *viejo* Park, the older one, and Will both stare daggers at him, before standing down. Will skips back to the tree line and starts looking around with Morgan. The *viejo* Park skips across to one end of the beach, and the two Parks studiously ignore one another while we work.

Although they cover the beach in a proper law enforcement grid in half the time, it is good for them not to know too much about each other's movements. In ignorance, you have freedom. Know too much about your future and you start feeling like a puppet, pulled by unseen strings. The only thing worse than that sinking feeling is the discord that comes from trying to change things.

The walking around and bending and shivering against the cold does me good. It is not very long from the rocks to the trees, only the length of about one block, a sliver of sand between some logs and the road to the campgrounds and the back bay. The footprints had been washed out below the tide line, but my ... the body is just barely past high tide.

There are two sets of bootprints, fresh, sizes 10W and 12, from halfway up the beach, stamping to the body and up to the tree line and back. They get all busy around the body. We also uncover, near the tree line, another set of bootprints, matching my hiking boots, walking up to three paces (and for me, a pace is two feet and eight inches) from the body. I apparently got that far, then things got very confused...or it could be that Will and I stupidly stamped it underfoot like *toros locos*.

In the pace or two around the body, there's cigarette butts half-smashed in the sand, including one of Will's Camels. And one none of us can identify.

"Over here," Morgan calls, "another set of tracks."

Both the Parks and I come over to look. At the edge of the high-tide line, there is a track - part of one. The front half of a bare footprint. A third man? Or a beachcomber? It would take two to kill the likes of me. Beyond that, there's nothing more to be found. One of the Parks nods to me, and skips away in a flash.

We slowly approach the body, where Will still stands, smoking a Camel.

"Detective Howe," Officer Park asks, "why in Hell are you stamping around a crime scene? We're lucky we can even identify there was a scuffle here."

Will clears his throat, his face stoic as an Active Service recruiting mnemonic. He's changed his accent and mannerisms, like a good Eternist, to match his surroundings…but at times like this, Will's English birth tells.

"It's not every day a friend dies." He says, quietly.

"And now that we've been fucking around here, I can't exactly bring in the Force." Park huffs. Both Will and Morgan start to sneer at the idea of mere police solving an Eternist's murder. "Laugh it up, guys, it's a murder of a Morro Bay resident on State lands. I do carry this fucking badge for a reason, y'know."

"You're an Eternist first," Morgan notes, "and an officer of the Temporal Security Bureau, as well as…"

"*Amigos*," I say, "I asked you here for a reason?"

The body we'd all been studiously ignoring draws our eyes again. Park's jaw goes slack, and he crouches down, peering at the body with those tight eyes. Suddenly, he makes a choking nose, and looks up at me.

"Ligature strangulation?" Park asks, his voice hoarse.

"Yes." I say, sipping my nearly-drained coffee.

Park and Morgan exchanged glances.

"What?" I ask.

Morgan reaches into his bag, and produces an unmarked evidence baggie. Suddenly, I am not hungry. I don't think I will ever eat again.

Inside the bag is the soft rainbow scarf Rachel was wearing last night.

II

April 20, 2014 – 7:13:32 AM

"*Madre de Diós.*"

We are all sitting in Morgan's black, mid-2000s Hummer. Morgan, Park, and Will have all finished their bagels and are sipping the dregs of their coffee. Morgan is smoking one of his Cuban cigars, tickling everyone's nose with the chocolaty smell of tobacco. Will has another Camel lit. The last of my coffee sits by going cold.

Outside, we watch another Morgan, another Park, as they lift another Gabriel, and in twin flashes, take him away. They return instantly, without the body, wearing different clothes, and clean up the beach. There have already been two cars passing in the last half-hour, and we want the beach clean before anyone else happens by.

No one has spoken for a while. I do not know how long.

"*Madre de Diós…*" I say again, "*no es possible.*"

Somehow, the sound coming out of my mouth brings me to. I notice the aches, the way I've slumped down in the seat, the warm metal weight of the Colt at my ribs, the barrel digging into my belly. My body and I, we are like *that*. We are tight. But not today. Today, I want to be a few millennia away.

"Maybe not," Park notes, boyish face turned back to Will and me in the backseat, "but you gotta admit, it's pretty suspicious."

"My senior, my *viejo*, dispatched it to me," Morgan said, butchering the pronunciation, "when he told me where I was to deliver it. He referred to it purely as 'the evidence.' I refrained from asking any details, just the time and place to show."

"It's *Rachel!*" I shout. I feel a pressure behind my eyes and red blood in them, and it has nothing to do with fatigue. "She is *mi amor*, she has not an evil bone in her body! I know her like I know myself. She is squeamish at butchering a chicken! She volunteers at the soup kitchen on Wednesdays! It cannot be her."

I am shouting, but it is hollow and unmanly. I know this voice. It is the voice of one of my clients, saying it is impossible his wife is sleeping around. It is the voice of a frightened character witness, who does not want to admit his friend could have done those things. It is the voice of a desperate man.

"Gooch," Morgan says, looking out to the bay, "you are seen with her at Legends. You argue. Loudly. Violently. She threatens to kill you. We can corroborate this, it happens."

Morgan's words are like a verbal slap to bring me to my senses. He's just told me point blank about my future. I want to demand what it is we argue about, but I know better. If I know too much of my own future, what do I become? A puppet. A mechanical man. When I was younger, the question would keep me awake at night. Now I mostly try not to think about it.

There are a lot of things I am trying not to think about.

"When?" I croak.

"Last night." Morgan says. His voice is even. Even through the back of his head, through the seat, I can picture his face. It is my face, when I must break the news of infidelity to the poor wife, or tell the children that their father is never coming home. "Between eight and ten thirty. Then you and she run home, with five witnesses."

"Hell of an argument." Park says, to no one in particular. Will doesn't seem to hear, but Morgan flicks his ash in the ashtray by way of dismissal. I do not mind, Matthew Park knows only how to tell jokes when he is upset. Will and I usually go drinking. We will need to, soon.

"And I die between two and four." I note.

"When was high tide?" Will blurts out. His voice is surprising, and I only now realize he hasn't spoken much. Morgan checks on his phone, laying the cigar in the ashtray while he does.

"2:36." He says.

"So between one and two-thirty."

While they are talking, my mind is whirring. It has the overheated, too-fast feel of living on coffee instead of sleep. "Why out here? There are better places to throw a body."

"Even for mundanes, yes." Will says, sitting next to me, his chin folded into his lap. He looks up, and notices the look I'm giving him. "Er, sorry, Gooch, no disrespect to her."

I just nod at him, quick and decisive, feeling the heat under my shirt collar cool off.

"You said the body was moved," Park confirms. "You're sure?"

"Livor mortis all around the…" I gesture on my own body, "but we found him face down."

Park nods. "So the placement was intentional. The killer must have known it'd be found."

"Found by us or by someone passing by?" I wonder aloud. "And moved from *when?*"

I can feel the attention in the car, even though the other three are all looking carefully away from me. Without speaking, they come to an agreement.

Humor the poor bastard, they're thinking. I do not need to be rank ten and equipped with mind-reading bugs to know this.

"Or where." Morgan adds finally, drumming his fingers on the wheel. "This is why I hate time-active cases."

"That's why you're California's only time-travelling lawyer, huh?" Park grins at him, that little-boy smirk. Morgan just glares back. "Bet your timesheets are something else."

"It cannot be Rachel." I insist. "It is not her."

"But it's got to be someone you know." Will insists. "You can't make a bunch of new enemies like that in just three days. Who else, besides Rachel, has a killing grudge against you?"

He looks at me with a glance I can feel in my gut.

"There is someone it could be." Morgan says, turning those flinty grey eyes on me. "Lightfoot's out on parole."

I do not blanche. I flush, feeling the blood rushing through my muscles. I want to run, to jump, to fight a man. My fists ball involuntarily.

Hank Lightfoot. The son-of-a-bitch that chased Debbie-Anne from Texas to California, who thought he was hot shit, who would have killed her...

Will squeezes my shoulder.

"I fought it as hard as I could," Morgan whispers, "kept him in as long as possible. But in the end, there wasn't anything I could do."

He sounded genuinely apologetic. Coming from Morgan, *mas gringo de los gringo*s, that was like a full sobbing confession from a lesser man.

"Is he still stripped at least?" I demand.

Park is the one who shakes his head this time.

"The county of San Luis Obispo has no charge left against him, so neither does Temporal Security." He admits. "He's still under the restraining orders you took out, at least."

But he's out…served his sentence…*Ay carumba* has it already been five years? Where does the time go?

"It is not very helpful to keep him a hundred feet away if he can just skip right up, is it?" I ask him. But I am not angry with him. Matthew Park, more than anyone else except maybe Will, gets it. He is a cop through and through, and he serves both the Twelve Laws of Time and the laws of Morro Bay, California…and he is *mi amigo* because he considers them equally important.

Men like Lightfoot? He thinks the laws that apply to Rachel and Debbie-Anne do not apply to him. He says to himself, "I am time-active. I am above such little things."

I am no saint. We all say it, sometimes, even me. As scrupulous as Morgan is about the Laws of Time, that is not his first Cuban cigar. I have known him to cheat timesheets, lie to the IRS, and fiddle with claims with a few timely skips. And I know this because we have drunk together at the café, and he is not ashamed to tell, among us.

He knows we all must break a few little laws, we who know too much about law, in order to do our jobs. He also knows that there are lines that he must not cross lest he find me heading a posse to collect him. And I know it works in reverse too. I am not always clean about how I use time.

But Lightfoot...*ay yai yai*, he is something else.

"Who's his officer?" I demand. His parole officer might be helpful...

"Harrison." Morgan notes. "I'll text you his number."

"I'm already on it, Gooch." Park says, the roundness of his cheeks belying the steel in his voice. "Don't you worry about Hank Lightfoot. I'll surveil him from here to the red line if it comes to that. Rendezvous at Legends, Friday night, seven o'clock. You and Will have bigger things to worry about."

I look out over the beach, about to ask what about the nexus, and suddenly think: *Chingao!* If it had not been my own body, I would have had out the notepad, the camera, my phone's recorder, gone over them all later for some proof tying it to Lightfoot. But we have been watching the whole time, and no Gooch showed up with these things. *Chingao*...I am a methodical man, an objective man. The more I feel on a case, the less good work I do, and this one...

...well, it's not every day a man handles his own murder.

"It would be his style." I say. "He is a passionate man. And this was a crime of passion."

Will nods.

"Strangling, defense wounds, semi-public location...this is someone violent. Someone unhinged. Not someone disciplined, controlled. Not someone like us." He says with finality. It is good to hear the certainty back in his voice, the old trustworthy iron. Here is a man, his voice says, you can trust with your daughter, your money, and your life.

Outside, in twin flashes, the other Morgan and other Park disappear. The beach is clean and fresh, just as the first joggers come running by. Rachel will be coming by here soon, on her own jog.

Rachel...

The scarf is still in Morgan's bag.

"I woke up on Friday morning," I say, "and I find out I am dead on Sunday morning. Easter Sunday, no less! In two days, I die. Nothing I do can stop Will from finding me on the beach. *Que será, será.*"

But perhaps I am not dead. Not yet. Perhaps I am just borrowing time...and Rachel need not be a widow. Yet. I will one day need to come back and die. But not yet. Nexus or no nexus, I might get out of this one.

This will require a delicate dance. I must find out who the bastard is, so Will can assemble a posse and give him what he deserves. Best of all would be right after he does the deed. But I cannot find out too much. The less I know of what happens on the beach on Easter morning, the more I can change what happens. I might even be able to change whether or not I die today, or whether I have to come back sometime down the line and do my duty.

Living on borrowed time is a small price to pay for another day with Rachel.

They are all looking at me. I have been quiet for some minutes. I look up at them, meet each of them in the eye with my *bravura*, and speak.

"What we can do," and I nod to Will, "is make sure the *cabrón* who did it comes to justice. *Our* justice."

I pat the Colt at my ribs. Morgan grins, a feral and fearsome thing, like an angry dog. He will enjoy this posse. Will's jaw throbs, as he does every time he must do a distasteful duty. Park takes a deep, slow breath, his nostrils flaring, and lets it out in a hiss from between his lips.

"It is not Rachel." I declare again. "I do not care what scarves you bring. She will not kill. Yes, she plays rough at rugby, fine. But kill? She cannot do it. It would not be difficult for one of us to lift the scarf, would it?"

I look around the car, and wonder who has been in the house enough to know where Rachel hangs her scarves. *Madre de Diós*, I thought I left this kind of paranoia behind when I left 1514.

"I need to talk to people," I say, "go down to the café."

A trip into San Luis, a trip to Linnaea's. Where information is carefully rationed, lest you see too much of your own future. Or because it might implicate someone's past.

"But first, I need sleep. I am not skipping around like this."

Sleep…and time with my family. I only have so much of either left.

Will and I open our eyes up the street from The Home of Gabriel Caballero y Gutiérrez and Rachel McCoy-Caballero, in the narrow mess of rakes and detritus between our red two-story and the fence. We are on the hill, so the location is shielded from view on every side. You might suspect it was this thing, more than the granny unit or the Great Recession pricing, that encouraged me to buy. You would be right.

Will's still shaken. Worse than I have ever seen. I throw one arm around him, and give him a little shake, *hermano y hermano.*

"I'll find him." I promise. "You lead the charge."

He tightens his jaw, and tries to smile at me. I give him a slug to the arm, and let go. I don't know if this is the last time we will see each other. I hope not. I grab his hand, feeling the calluses and the strength, and shake it, once. We nod at each other. When I let go, he is gone, in a quiet flash of light.

I take a deep breath, and look to the shadows. It's about eight in the morning, back on Friday. For once, my life is working in sync with the hours of the day.

I have two more breakfasts with my wife before I am dead on the beach. I want this one to count. I take a deep breath, feeling my ribs expand. There is power there, blood and life. I can feel it radiating off Rachel's limbs, off her skin, almost as if it is my own…why do we need to be ripped apart? And on Easter Sunday?

Her Prius is there, out in front of the garage, next to my old Toyota truck. We keep the bicycles in the garage. Along with the kayak, the equipment for whatever sport is not in season, her weight set, and a couple of things I have never been able to identify.

I debate checking on Amá (as we call our mothers in Jalisco) out in the back. No. It can wait until after breakfast. She is probably still

in bed. Besides, Francesca survived long enough without me. She is
not the one I am worried about.

The wood of the door is hard against my fingers. I have never
gotten used to how wood feels here. It's too slick and finished. After
alerting the girls, I open up.

"Hun?" Rachel's voice, to the right, from the kitchen. "Is that
you?"

"Lucy, I'm home!"

Don't look at me like that. I am Hispanic and I married a *loca*
redhead. We dated to the reruns, and we took it as our own.

She's already dressed, a little heavy for a late spring day at work,
all swishy skirts and a long-sleeve. I have to wonder at that. It's not
like the health food store disapproves of her tattoo. She has her
bronze hair tied in twin braids under a kerchief. Her full little mouth
is set, the angel's bow compressed to a straight line. She's holding a
plate of biscuits and gravy…oh, she made whole-wheat sourdough, *ay
yai yai* that *aroma*…and for a moment her brown eyes flash hard at me.

"Sorry I'm late, Rachel." I say, hanging up my coat by the door.

I shrug out of my holsters and hang them under the coat. My
wife has Opinions about guns. One of them is that I do not wear
them in her house. On the next peg, looking innocent as anything, is
Rachel's rainbow scarf. Her weapon, hanging by the door, right next
to mine.

She comes around the breakfast bar, and passes close by the
front door. I lean in to kiss her. She slides out of my reach, an
impressive feat of grace for an overgrown tomboy like her.

"Gabriel! I'm carrying breakfast..." she chides. She is joking, but I can hear the deeps behind it. It is a little like watching a clown perform on a boat when sharks are circling.

She sets down her plate next to the coffee cup. There's a second plate already laid out for Debbie-Anne.

There's no third plate.

I look up from the breakfast bar. Her voice is serious. "Where were you?"

"Morgan got a midnight call. He wanted me to see a character witness who flew out a few minutes ago." They are sweet and light, my words, like my mother's flan. I hate them.

The lies. Always the *lies*. The Sixth Law of Time makes us all damned liars. But I cannot tell her the truth...I know my woman, she could not hold it, and the choices for how to handle someone who knows...well, they get less nice as you go. I have had to go on cleanup a few times myself.

My woman, she does not show weakness. She will rant, and scream, and disappear into a book, and force her body to go to the point of death, but she will not tremble or cry. To tremble would be beneath her. But she just looks at me, her lower lip rolling under the teeth she thinks she is hiding with her upper lip. Then she turns to the stairs and shouts.

"Breakfaaast!" She is so loud I am afraid she will wake Amá. "Come an' git it!"

"Jesus Christ, Rach!" Debbie-Anne's response is just as loud, but slurred with sleep. "Gimme a minute! You sound like *Ma!*"

I stride into the kitchen to make myself some eggs. She does not look at me. I do not look at her. I am debating how I want my *huevos* when I see the bowl, with the little red kerchief left haphazard on top of it. I pull the cloth back, to reveal half a dozen half-whole wheat sourdough biscuits, and the full bread aroma blooms in my face. Rachel has sat down at the breakfast bar, sitting up straight, looking too tall by half. She is sipping her coffee. Our eyes meet, and hers flick to the saucepan. The gravy is still warm.

She did not know when I would come home. And it killed her. But she left warm gravy and fresh biscuits for me when I did come home. And that kills me.

My eyes are wet. Rachel must have been chopping onions...the scent must still in the air, tickling my nose. Yes. That's it. It takes me a minute to collect myself. I cover my grief by putting my biscuits and gravy together, taking time to do it up nice, and by pouring myself a cup of coffee. My favorite mug, from the health food store. *Caffe con leche.* Milk. Sugar.

In three days, Rachel will be alone.

I am not hungry, but a man does not learn to travel through time without taking meals at odd occasions to him. This meal, I would not miss it for all the gold in El Dorado or all the tea in China or all the secrets of the Legion. I set my plate down at the empty place while Rachel keeps sipping her coffee.

Without a word I clap my hand on Rachel's shoulder, like I would one of my brothers. She doesn't respond. I know she is truly angry...otherwise, she would be touching me back.

Ay yai yai, the lies...

I sit down to my silent breakfast. Why isn't she tearing into me? It's not like her to sit and stew.

"C'mn," Debbie-Anne announces, tromping down the stairs, blond curls askew, angel face still thick with sleep, wrist brace standing out against her pale skin. She's wrapped in one of her sister's robes, and it trails out behind her like a *quinceañera* dress. She stops for a moment, while we turn to her. Our faces are not yet set, and what has passed between us is still in the air. Even Debbie-Anne can pick it up. "'mah inneruptin'?"

Anyone else, Rachel would be smiling, "getting ready to interact proper," she likes to say. Her face doesn't change, looking at Debbie-Anne, but there are little movements, gestures between them. Debbie-Anne comes and sits down.

She is flighty and *loca*, and she cannot hold a boyfriend or a job to save her life (believe me when I say this), but we both love Debbie-Anne. She is one of the people Rachel can simply sit in a room with, and I can count the rest on one hand. I like her because she has the same *caritas* as her sister, and because we are both ... well, not so intellectual as Rachel can be.

And she knows when to break a conversation.

"*Whole wheat*, sugah?" Debbie-Anne asks, with that honey-coated voice McCoy women use to cover the arsenic. "You've been out here in California too long. What's in the gravy? Tofu and tahini?"

"Well, bless your heart," Rachel has turned up her accent, or maybe she is just mimicking her sister, "but I'm afraid I was all out of cola and Bisquick this morning. Some of us can actually get up early enough to *make* breakfast, not just eat it."

She smiles a prim little smile at Debbie-Anne. Debbie-Anne responds by sticking her tongue out, all grey and brown from breakfast. Rachel replies with the same. Debbie-Anne giggles like a schoolgirl, and Rachel gives her a tired little smile.

·Ah, of course. She is holding it in because Debbie-Anne is here. And it's eating her…

…there's no way she can know that she'll be widowed by Easter. I look into my biscuits and gravy, that my loving wife made against the hour that I come back. They taste like cardboard.

In three days, she will make biscuits and gravy, or *huevos rancheros*, or some strange Japanese thing, and I will never eat it. I will never come home to her couscous'n'grits, her (free-range) fried chicken and (organic) mashed potatoes, her red beans and rice, her after-workout high, her rasslin', her wide-eyed discovery, her righteous mania, her pale pale skin, her sweat, her hips, her kisses…

Sangre de Christo.

Would she act differently if she knew? Would she kiss me and sign off her kiss with a nibble of my lip? Would she hold me and let me stroke down one side of her backbone before she goes off to Sunshine? Would she even bother going to work?

…or would it be just the same?

Chingao! All these secrets…it feels like a force under my skin, pushing out, like I'm full up with secrets ready to spill over. I want to tell her, want her to know, want her to be prepared, but then that would lead to other questions and … I do not want her to forget.

Like I said, there are a lot of things I try not to think about any more. My throat cries for a shot of tequila.

Debbie-Anne is talking about what she's doing today, shopping trips and the beach, but her eyes dart between her sister and me. We eat in silence, and let her talk.

"You can use my Prius." Rachel finally replies. "Just drop me off at work first."

Rachel, being Rachel, usually takes her bike to Sunshine. Debbie-Anne, being Debbie-Anne, cannot imagine taking a five-minute walk to the beach when she could drive instead. Also, I realize with a bitterness that I can taste, it gives them a chance to talk without me around.

"Wait, girls." I say, sipping the last dregs of my *caffe con leche.* "Something you two should know. My lawyer friend, Morgan, he lost his appeal. Hank Lightfoot's out on parole."

Debbie-Anne startles as a ghost of her past rears its ugly head. I can't blame her. Rachel is caught by complete surprise.

"The restraining orders are still in effect, and I have his parole officer's number." I say. "You see him, even walking down the street, you can call 911."

Debbie-Anne is trembling like a leaf now. I stand, and give her a big Mexican hug.

"You're safe, Debbie-Anne." I tell her. "You're still safe. But I thought you should know."

I feel her calm down under my arms, and let her go. Rachel is just watching, stewing.

I promise it is not normally like this. Normally, when Rachel is angry, *Ai yai yai*, you know it. When Debbie-Anne is visiting, we are the three *amigos*. But I cannot tell her, and she knows I am lying, and we can't fight in front of Deborah Anne McCoy. It seems wrong, even to me.

When Rachel gets up, I reach out for her one more time. She shakes her head once, quickly, tersely.

"Not now, Gabriel." She says, and her eyes finally do meet mine. "But I have words to mince with you."

The honey-brown eyes flash something at me. Something intense and passionate…and hateful. It is like a bullet to my chest, and I draw back. And she walks out of my reach. I go and stand by the unlit fireplace and curse mentally in Spanish until I hear the door close.

When I turn around, I am looking into my own face: the 'framed picture' mouth, the Habsburg chin, the twinkling eyes and goat-curl hair. I've changed, a fresh button-down, khakis, chukkas. Bluetooth in my ear. Over one shoulder, a sport coat, and in the other, a briefcase I know has a tie in it, along with the other tools of my trade: the disposable razors, the toothbrush, the binoculars and listeners and yellow legal pads.

"How long?" I ask, in the Spanish of Jalisco.

"About four hours." He replies, in the same tongue. He sounds…confident. All together. Like he knows what he's doing. It helps, knowing I will be like that soon. I focus on him, remembering each movement and inflection…in four hours, I must become him. "Enough to get business done. Sleep, *señor*. I will check on Amá."

He leaves me be. I hear the door open again, close again. Then I lay my forehead up against the wall a minute, before I stumble to the daybed in my office.

III

April 18, 2014 – 9:03:44 AM

Madre de Diós, I felt like shit. After my nap, I pack the briefcase for a long day's work and have a shot to steady my nerves. Long day…long couple of days. I only have two days to live all my time and find that bastard and make sure he pays for what he does to me. Upstairs, I shower and dress and make myself presentable. Already, I feel more like Gabriel Caballero y Gutiérrez, fifth rank, licensed detective, husband of Rachel McCoy, a *caballero* good and true. I test myself by skipping back four hours from the office, arriving just after Rachel and Debbie-Anne left.

I was standing against the fireplace, looking already dead, like *la Llorna* is already come and I have invited her in for coffee. I turn around, and I am looking myself in the face again. Robust, with brown eyes like Jalisco earth and skin the color of Rachel's morning mocha. But the shoulders are already folded, the head slumped forward like my chin is filled with shot.

A nap, a shower, and a shot of tequila will do wonders for a man.

"How long?" He asks, in the Spanish of Jalisco.

"About four hours." I say in the same tongue. The memory of being him is creeping into me, but I fight to keep it out of my voice. I must believe I know what I am doing, in my future.

Shift my camel's-hair coat, like so. Cock-eyed smile. I like it, it is why I use it in front of *las mujeres*, in front of Rachel. She likes it too.

"Enough to get business done." I say. I let the corner of my mouth fall, as I remember seeing. I let my voice become soft, brotherly. "Sleep, *señor*. I will check on Amá."

He nods, but his eyes are still stunned with the fresh wound of Rachel's glance. *Ay carumba*...I do not want to remember. I leave him be, don my holsters, and lock the front door when I go.

Amá calls out in Jalisco Spanish when I knock on her door. Her door is up a set of outside stairs behind the main house...only a bedroom and kitchen and the sitting room, but she has the back yard. She gardens by touch, growing the vegetables she always disdained back home in the village of Belaños, long ago.

My baby sister, Francesca, is 93 this year. Time has perhaps mellowed her strong head.

I call out "Amá," and open the door.

Francesca is listening to music, the flamenco of our Spanish cousins, and trying to follow on a guitar in her hands. The nylon shivers under her fingers...her hand is weathered, but her grip is still strong. They breed Caballeros for strength.

I wait until she is finished, until her song has run its course. It is a bad idea to interrupt Francesca...time has not mellowed her strong head so much as all that.

"Francesca, my auntie," I say, hitting the pause button, "how is the music coming?"

"Not so bad," she replies, "but *ay carumba* I don't know if a Mexican *paisana* can quite manage all that Spanish complexity!"

"Don't worry, Amá..." I pause. The next words out of my mouth were almost "I remember..." but as far as Francesca knows, I am the son of her beloved brother. Even after four years, I find it hard to lie to her. "...my father always told me you could not be stopped, even when all the saints on Earth and angels in Heaven were holding you back."

Francesca's smile looks a lot like mine. That is sensible, her chin, her jaw, her framed-picture mouth, her nose, they are like mine. But the white cataracts, wide as lanterns, are not like mine, and neither is the brow furrowed by years of frustration and disappointment.

The lines are clearing though. They have been, these four years. I have not looked her up in the 2030s to see what becomes of her. I like having some pleasant surprises in my life. That is why Francesca is here. That is why Rachel is here.

"And you," she asks, resting her hand and the lace of her sleeve on the unvarnished body of the guitar, "how is your *gringa*?"

In the names of Mary and Joseph, she is blind but I swear she can still see me turn my head away. Even after four years, I find it hard to lie to my sister.

"It is hard." I admit. "I have to keep a lot from her, and you know these *gringas*, they don't like that."

She barks a sharp, warm laugh.

"*Gringas* are all *locas*," she says, "but that one, I think she is *loca* like you."

I want to ask what she means, but her head bows to her guitar, and the strings begin to dance again. Francesca used to dance, in the firelight of the hacienda, when the boys all walk one way, the girls all walk the other. Even then, it was always with a Caballero's strength and honor, deep into the night, and a Caballero's joking, always with a half-grin.

The music of her guitar is the dance of her youth…the girl lives on in the crone.

I say, "Goodbye, Amá," and let myself out. It is time for me to work, and when Gabriel Caballero works, no secrets are safe.

The Prius is gone, but my truck remains. It is a little battered, gunmetal grey Japanese import from 1982. Nothing can kill it, and I have had several people try, so I know. I throw my briefcase on the passenger seat when I get in, and lay the sport coat on top of it.

A detective must have a car, with its shotgun, its dusty fingerprint kit under the driver's seat, its collection of hats and sunglasses, its wide-mouthed jar. *Tristemonte*, it is now April, and the camper shell would be too suspicious, but I have made great use of that, as well. It is easy to surveil for two days straight when you can take a break whenever you want. A rank five should not be able to carry several tons of Japanese engineering through time, but I filed my papers and got help from *mis patrónes* Will and Morgan.

I start the beast, and hear it purr. I have met *la Malinche* and fought with Pelayo against the Moor. I have watched my apartment open at the brush of my fingers and say hello in a sultry voice. I have lost my breath at the sparkling rainbow reflections of New York City's Bomb Inlet. But I am still impressed and pleased with the simple power of an oil engine, purring at me, my seat trembling. It is still a wonder to me, who grew up with horses and carriages like you see in the Zorro movies, that such power is underneath my feet.

And it always makes me chuckle that *gringo*s never seem to notice.

I pull out of Sundancer Village, and slide directly onto Quintana Boulevard, heading for the roundabout and out of town. I make the first call on my Bluetooth while pulling onto Highway 1 going south. I only have two days, I cannot be spending time on other jobs...for once, I am living according to the detective fictions, working all my day on The Big Case. First I call my two lawyer clients, one I was going to meet with at one o'clock and one who wants me to find his missing witness, then I call Polk Insurance and tell them I cannot look into the arson case in Atascadero tomorrow. More calls, to explain delays and missed appointments. I reschedule everything for after Easter.

After Easter I will either be dead, or God in his Heaven will grant another miracle.

The café I'm going to is in San Luis Obispo, maybe twelve or fifteen miles to the south. It's called Linnaea's, and it exists from 1984 until sometime in 2046, the middle shop on the ground floor of a large, old facade that rambles with stately small-town pride across the entire block. In all that time, it is host to artists, students, scholars, strange peoples of all kinds. There is a beautiful garden in the back that it shares, in 2014, with a hairdresser next door. Rachel likes to stop there when she's going to town.

It is also the social center of all time-active activity in San Luis Obispo from 1984 until 2046. Who do you think approved the original bank loan? Conventional entrance to "the café" as we mean it isn't the café itself, but the stairs next door into the Maino Building, and the offices and apartments set up on the next two stories over Linnaea's. But unless there are visitors from a long time off or other selves coming, most of our business happens in Linnaea's itself. The coffee is good and so is the mood.

When I pass the light at Cuesta College, maybe halfway to San Luis Obispo, my brain turns to the question at hand. Tomorrow night, Rachel and I will fight. Sometime after midnight, I am on the campground stretch of beach. In two days, my dead body is found there. I am strangled, and the murder weapon is presumed to be my wife's scarf. I fight my killer, or killers, and die on my back, facing them, like a man. My best suspect is Hank Lightfoot, a man of hot blood and vicious ways who likes to see his women bruised and broken. Or it might be someone else. Because it cannot be Rachel.

I think back to her last glance, to her coldness.

...can it?

Two days is Easter Sunday, when Christ rose again. Two days is a nexus. A nexus is a time when there are a lot of time-actives all around, so every skip becomes a little bit dangerous. They happen around big events, like Easter, 33AD in Jerusalem, like October 12, 1492 on the shores of Hispaniola, like August 31, 1946, Hiroshima, but they can also happen just because of the weight of the time-actives around. You are liable to skip away, and fall down with a bump because you are two feet off the ground, or come out one mile from where you wanted to be. Or never come out at all. You must be careful. It is a little like driving through a heavy storm, or driving through a light rain if you are a *gringo*.

I need to find out who knocked on Will's door. I need to find out when and where Lightfoot is, in as much detail as possible...I want to know when he hits me and when he goes after that, so Will,

Morgan, and Park can meet him there. I need to find out how bad a nexus it is. I need to find out what it is I don't know.

Chingao, I wish I had brought camera and notebook. Already details are slipping away.

But these are time-actives, and not all of us are nice. Information, among us, is everything. You can control a man by controlling his knowledge and his ignorance. I have done this many times in my career...tell a man his lover spoke to you, and he will go to call her. Do not tell a woman what she wants to know, and you will see what kind of woman she is. It is a trade tool of a private investigator.

The information I want will come with a price. It always does. I have been a good detective so far because I know what my information is worth and how to haggle like an Indian at the Belaños market. But this time, I do not have enough information to trade with, and must go begging. Just as cause must always lead to effect, one favor has to repay another, or it all comes crashing down.

That is all right. Perhaps I will have the knowledge they need, but not yet. And they know I will have the knowledge I need, even if not yet. I never said talking to time-actives was easy.

Aside from the four or five of us in the Morro Bay contingent, there are maybe fifty or sixty regulars scattered across the county throughout time, plus visitors. There are a dozen or two dozen who are regulars at the café. Uncle Jerry will be there, and Alison Wingate III, and dreamy little Erin, and Lawrence and the Australian sapling.

I park the truck on a little residential street, nestled next to the old water works over San Luis Creek, because they do not have parking meters and it is only a few blocks to Garden Street and Linnaea's Café.

As I'm turning off Higuera, onto Garden, Uncle Jerry waves. He's sitting at the open window, facing the street. He's a big man, in every way: big gut, big shoulders, big arms, big grizzly beard, big ponytail. It's almost funny to see his great big mitts fiddling with a delicate teacup. But I know better than to make assumptions, this man has saved my life with delicate fingers in my coat pocket more than once. I wave back, and cross the street.

"Gooch," he rumbles.

"*Hola*," I tell him, "how's business?"

Uncle Jerry is a member of the local Bill-and-Teds, for time-actives who are too busy or too scattered to remember to slip the essential item in his pocket before he needs it. Instead of going back and doing it yourself, you ask Uncle Jerry to go do it for you, then go about your day. You find the pen – or the gun – or whatever you wanted – right when you need it, and Uncle Jerry has a little more knowledge to trade.

"Not bad," he admits, his face rocking back and forth in the mass of beard and hair as he nods. "Not bad."

"Getting busier?" I ask. If anyone will know about the nexus, it is Uncle Jerry.

He shakes his head.

"Not for the immediate future," he says, "but I expect things to pick up later. Pretty cagey question, Gooch. You here on business or is this a social trip?"

"*Eyyyy, amigo,*" I say, sounding hurt, "can't a man come to his usual café to see his *amigos* without it being assumed he has come with some ulterior motive?"

I smile at him. He smiles back.

"Thought so." He chuckles into his green tea. "Big case?"

"You could say so," I admit, "but I must solve it by Easter."

The cup stops halfway to his mouth. Slowly, it lowers back to the weathered wood counter.

"Ah." He says at last. "That case."

I nod.

"That case." I say. "You know?"

"Yeah...yeah, I heard what happened. C'mon upstairs. There's some people you need to talk to."

He waves to the barista, and takes the shop's teacup out with him. They know he will bring it back. He always does. We don't speak again until we have gone next door, into the Maino Building. The building has been here since the 1920s, I think, and always has the feel of being encased in amber. There is something timeless about the building. That is fitting.

We go up the inside steps, to the second story, and make a right. Behind a door with a pebble-glass window, we can hear voices. I hear *el Australiano*, and Alison, and a third voice, a woman's. Erin? Jerry looks around the deserted hall, and disappears in a polite little flash. I follow him in with a blink.

I open my eyes and look around. The foyer looks the same as always, nicely unassuming and normal, opening into two halls down to the bathrooms, bedrooms, and little offices for transacting transtemporal business. With a secretary, it would look exactly like a doctor's office. The only tells are the identical hampers and the schedules on the wall outlining who is responsible for laundry and when visitors are expected. My name is on the visitor's list, for eleven on Friday.

Alison and *el Australiano* are still talking, as if two men did not just appear from thin air in their midst. Alison Wingate III looks a bit like how my wife will be as an older woman, all bold patterns and tie-dye colors and cotton and leather and clinky "native" jewelry and smiles. She has the presence that comes with her blue blood, and a *doña*'s sense of justice. The *Australiano* is a thin little man, still green at the ears, with nervous hands that are always moving.

Between them, in an easy-chair, is the woman.

She's olive-colored, with dark hair, dark eyes, and care lines worn down her cheeks. She's watchful, wary, letting Alison and *el Australiano* swirl around her. Something about her makes me think of alley cats, something in her watchfulness, in her tiny underfed body, in her suspicious glances. She's wrapped in a red cocktail dress from the last century that's been ripped, abraded, and slept in. Next to her is a thin coat; that has also been ripped, abraded, and slept in. Her left shoe is damp at the toe. This one has a story to tell, I can feel it.

"But I don't know what happens to them," Alison is saying, "and neither do you."

"The fact that we don't know anything about them," *el Australiano* replies, "already tells us something. It's not like they amount to anything."

"It tells us no Laws of Time get broken if we feed a few unfortunates!" Alison insists. "They're suffering, and we can help them."

"Alison," *el Australiano* sniffs, "I would go mad if I tried to rescue everyone, and doubly so if I tried to rescue everyone while keeping the Twelve Laws intact. What you're saying is madness."

"It is not for you to decide who lives and who dies." The woman says. Her accent and her lisp place her immediately: Spanish. No no, not what you are thinking, *Spain* Spanish. But what is she doing here? And why have I not met her before? "Just because you can play with time does not mean you are God."

Whoever she is, I like her already. *El Australiano* sighs, shaking his head.

"Bunch of madwomen…Good morning, Gooch," he says. "Glad you're here."

That is not good.

"Our PI buddy here's looking for a lead on his case." Uncle Jerry rumbles. He and *el Australiano* exchange glances. *El Australiano* gestures me to a chair. The Spaniard remains in hers, her suspicious eyes on me as if she is trying to remember something.

"Gooch, you know we can't just tell you the events of your personal future, no matter how long or short it is."

I shake my head. I am more scrupulous about such things than this Australian. I know.

"That's fine." I say, waving it off. "I am not going to ask about me. I am going to ask about Lightfoot."

Alison's white brows shoot up her face.

"He's loose?" She asks. "In real-time?"

"And Will and Park unlocked him." I confirm. "Park's on his trail, but I need to know. Do we know when or where he is?"

"Well!" Alison huffs. "I certainly hope not. I don't want to be anywhere within a hundred days of him."

So he's not in the vicinity at present. We time-actives, we stick together…even men like Lightfoot. If he hasn't broken the Laws of Time, he is still usually acceptable among us, although the schedules become complicated as people arrange so that he and I do not meet. His name is nowhere on the visitor's sheet. So, he is either running, or he is hiding and biding his time. Perhaps he only knows when and where I will be that night, and does not know my movements until then. If so, it's because…

"Jerry," I say, "have you gotten any orders from Lightfoot? Professionally, I mean."

He shakes his head.

"I'll give that one to ya, I ain't seen hide or hair of him." He looks at me with an unspoken 'yet' in his stonewashed blue eyes.

"Call me if you talk to him." I say. Uncle Jerry nods.

"You're not the only one asking around after blokes." *El Australiano* says. "Hector's been looking for you."

"Hector?" I ask, brow furrowing.

"Descanso." *El Australiano* confirms. "Says he knows you from the '30s."

He unconsciously thumbs upwards. The 2030s, then; my journeyman years in the detective trade. That is very funny…I need to look at my case files at home, or the case files I left in 2036, see if I can place him.

"And what has he been asking about me?" I ask.

"Where you are," the Australian replies, "when you are. Whether you've seen mutual acquaintances recently."

Someone is trying to surveil me? This is essentially what I am trying to do to Hank Lightfoot…know what he is doing, when is the earliest that a posse could come for him. I can't but wonder if this is the same reason why Hector Descanso wants me measured… measured for a pressboard box.

And still, the little Spaniard watches everything. She misses nothing. Speaking as one of them, there is something dangerous about such people.

"Which acquaintances?"

"A Chinese woman. Jessica Huang." Alison lilts the name a little, because she speaks Chinese.

Now the pieces fall into place. I knew Hector Descanso as an informant, the kind of time-active who never collects his big score because he loves the hustle a bit too much. Hector was a tiny Asian man, and when I knew him he was a grifter and not yet one of us. He did me good favors, and when his time came, I voiced my approval when Jessica wanted to give him the *cabaceo*, the invitation to tango through time.

Why would he be surveilling me? Why now? It is something in my life that is important to him…but what am I doing in 2014 that is important to a small-stakes grifter who is not even born yet?

Ai yai yai. More mysteries.

"Have we..." The Spaniard narrows her eyes at me. "...met yet?"

It takes me a moment to realize she has addressed me in Spanish. Now I can place her: Catalonian, somewhere in the east of Spain. Barcelona, maybe. A proud race, the Catalans.

"No," I reply in Spanish, shaking my head, "I don't recognize your face. And I would. It is a pretty face."

Her lips tighten and widen, but she cannot hide the smile completely. More than anything, it is amusement.

"Your entrance into my life is something I will remember for a long while." She says.

Ah. This kind of thing happens all the time. She has met me, I have not met her. When I have met her, she has not met me. The *gringo*s call it a Claire, I do not know why. I look over her dress, very obviously.

"You look like you have a story to tell." I comment. She shakes her head.

"Our..." Uncle Jerry searches for the word, and I don't think it's because he's bad with Spanish, "...guest is suffering from retrograde amnesia."

Remember I said it can be dangerous to skip in a nexus? That is one of the reasons. I look to her, she nods.

"I remember," she says in English, "waking up on gravel near running water. It was dark." She pauses. "It was very dark. That was last night. It was very cold. And very wet. Like the..."

She is hunting for the word, and can only find it in Spanish. She switches back to it. "...like the *mistral*. And I remember Barcelona...Mama and Papa."

The corners of her mouth turn down, digging into her cheeks. It makes her look even more like a little girl grown old before her time.

"I don't remember anything in between." That Barcelona must have been a long time ago. She has uttered five whole sentences without cursing. I know no modern Spaniards who can do this.

"Consider yourself hired, Gooch." Uncle Jerry says, in gutter Spanish. "I don't know about the rest of these skips, but I can tell you that working out this young lady's dilemma will get you a long way toward solving your own case. A *long* way."

"She'll owe me a favor, huh?"

"Might be a bit more than that." He chuckles, raspy and throaty.

"Something in her past?"

"Ask your *viejo*." He says. Ask my senior: Discussion closed.

He is looking at me with that glint in his eye. So he knows how this turns out and will not say, huh? This must be how it feels when I talk to, say, someone buying real estate in Morro Bay in 2006. Or considering stocks in early September of 1929.

I have things to do, I want to shout at him. I have that rendezvous with Park over his Lightfoot investigation, I have Hector to worry about, and I have to play pussyfoots with my knowledge of what happens on Easter morning. And if it's not the investigation, I'd rather be with my wife...I will go to her rugby game and eat dinner with her and Amá and Debbie-Anne after. It won't help my investigation but I challenge you to do differently in my place. A man must have his family; when he is facing the gun, more than any other time.

Jerry watches me. He knows what I am thinking, and what I will say. Played into a corner. *Ai yai yai* as if I do not have enough to do...

"All right," I say, through gritted teeth. "I will get her home."

"I am sitting right here," she says automatically, steel sliding into her voice as if from a scabbard, "you don't need to talk about me as if I didn't exist. I may have memory problems but I am fully conscious and capable of choosing my own *patrón*, or none, thank you very much."

Our eyes meet. Something in her eyes makes me blink. They are the dark eyes of a killer, a veteran or a survivor...eyes that have seen terror and blood and cannot drive them too far from the here and now. She carries a burning Barcelona there, behind her eyes. It is not what I expected to see in her.

Even with all the secrets of time travel, some things are still inexplicable, still magic. *La bomba* is one of them. I cannot say how I know, but I know this woman is all tangled up in my life, and I am all tangled up in hers.

"You are right." I stammer. "I apologize."

Alison and el *Australiano* have waited patiently, but Alison is fiddling with her wooden bead necklace and the Australian is tugging at his nonexistent beard. Briefly, Jerry explains the conversation that just happened.

"May I help you find your way home, *señorita?*" I ask. "Do you know your name?"

"María Ortega y Carerra." She says. She does not extend a hand. She is not from a time when women shook hands. "We did not have the opportunity this morning. And yes. I would appreciate that greatly."

I frown a little. You aren't supposed to fill up a person's schedule like that…it's rude, it reminds us how little choice we have, moving through time. I replace the frown with a pleasant smile, and remind myself I am speaking to a client.

"Gabriel Caballero y Gutiérrez." I say, giving her my hand. "A pleasure to meet you."

She raises one eyebrow, and puts her hand in mine. Her palm is horny with calluses, her knuckles are scarred. The scars are all old and faded. She has seen fights, but now knows some peace.

"Caballero, hm?" She says, as I kiss her scarred knuckles. She has that sardonic smile again. "Then rescuing the ladies is your business."

I think of Debbie-Anne. I think of Rachel. She withdraws her hand.

"You could say that." I say, running my hand over my face. "So how did you come here? How did you know to get here?"

Uncle Jerry presents a card. On the back is Linnaea's address, written in Spenserian hand. Old-fashioned. On the front is an appointment for the Old Barber Shop in Morro Bay, in high July of 1958. In my business, this is what we call a clue.

Since my marriage, I have not been so good as Will about practicing my skipping, about playing with time. Some time-actives insist it is like yoga or dancing, that kind of connection. I have not felt it. 1958 is a bit outside what I can do. I turn the card back over.

"You followed the address on the card, hmm?" I ask, showing it to her. María nods. "What happened then?"

"Go see for yourself." Alison says. "You were there."

"When?" I ask, standing up.

"You said three hours, twelve minutes, and thirty-six seconds." Alison reports. Some of us need notebooks. Alison does not.

I nod. 1958 is too far for me, but this morning? That I can do. I think about it, and blink.

The room's light is different. Fresher. And it's instantly cooler, as I return to a time when San Luis Obispo had not completely shaken the damp April dawn.

"…good morning, Gooch?" I hear the pleasant, absent voice in stereo. Alison with herself, carrying breakfast in from downstairs. She looks at me bleary-eyed.

"Three hours, twelve minutes, and thirty-six seconds." I say. She nods, white mug bobbing, trusting this information will be useful later.

Jerry is there, stretched on a couch and reading Jack London, looking like he has had a long night about a century away. He's all leather and denim, not like the Uncle Jerry I just left in his t-shirt and jeans. A different day, a different Jerry. We nod to one another.

That's when we hear the weak tap of someone knocking on the pebbled glass. Alison looks at herself and one of her vanishes into the quiet light of time. The remaining Alison steps forward and opens the door a crack.

"We're not open for…" She starts. "…oh."

She looks around, then opens the door for María Ortega y Carerra. She looks like Hell, covered in smudge and stains and dirt and, in some places, caked blood. Doesn't smell so nice either. The tiny Spaniard is trembling, afraid, her dark, bloodshot eyes darting around as if she expected every shadow to jump at her.

"Is this…" she starts in Spanish. "What is this place?"

Killer's eyes, maybe, but right now she is mostly just a frightened alley cat. The others, though, they are hard-eyed, guarded. Glances fly around the room like radio signals.

"A place where you are safe." I tell her. "Our safe-house."

"Gooch, are you sure we can let in a-" I silence Alison with a glance. I want to tell her that of course the Spaniard speaks English and not to talk about her that way.

"Trust me." I tell her. "This is María Ortega y Carerra, from Barcelona, Spain. She's my client."

I gesture for her to come in. She hesitates, she has trusted 'the kindness of strangers' before. But she acknowledges that she is out of options, and steps forward with determination, into the warm foyer. "Have we met yet?" I ask.

She looks at me oddly, as if she doesn't understand. I nod to Alison, who shuts the door. María's still trembling, clinging to the front of her dress. I reach out, slowly, and feel her cheek. It's chilly. She does not draw back, but she does meet my gaze.

"*Señorita,*" I tell her, "there is a washroom through that hallway and on your left. It has a shower and a toilet, plenty of hot water. Are there towels and things?"

We all look to Uncle Jerry. He rolls his eyes and nods, taking out
a notebook to place the order. In his future, he makes sure that
towels and so on are in the washroom at this moment.

"But first, are you hungry?" I ask. "Have you had breakfast?"

She shakes her head.

"I'll grab you some." I tell her. "Just a moment."

"*Graci-*"

I blink.

Twenty minutes before, Alison is just emerging from one of the
guest rooms. She nods to me at the door while I go downstairs. The
morning is chilly and damp in my shirtsleeves, *ay carumba* and María is
wandering through this with only that light dress? I buy a black
Spanish coffee and a cup of the barley soup to warm up the poor
señorita. With the bowl and coffee in hand, I walk out to the garden,
still glistening with dew, deserted in the chill. I make sure no one is
looking, and skip back.

"*-as.*" Is just coming out of her mouth when I reappear. Then,
she screams.

Alison's eyes go wide as eggs. She stands before her and puts
one finger up between her eyes.

"Sleep." She commands. An Erikson induction, designed to
confuse the brain into following orders, and the orders come
flooding forth from Alison in her nice, grandmotherly voice.

Jerry is up on his feet, ready for anything. Slowly, the little
Spaniard calms down. Alison takes her by the hand, leading her into
the hall. I set down the uneaten breakfast.

"…and you can just come out when you're done with your shower, miss." She finishes. The bathroom door closes.

Alison turns on me with a terrible look in her eye.

"Did someone decide there are only Eleven Laws of Time now and nobody tells me?" She demands.

"Gooch, *what the hell?*" Jerry demands. "Alison, you're going to need to do cleanup."

"I can wait until she's washed and fed." Alison shivers. "It breaks my heart there are people wandering around like that. But Gooch, what were you *thinking* skipping in front of a mundane?"

That word again. I do not take kindly to time-actives using that word, and Alison knows this. Jerry is no stranger to *amarse un lio*, and he steps back while I square off with Alison. This is not his fight. I can feel my back coming up, even against Alison.

"She's one of us," I growl, a little harsher than I meant to. "In three hours she's sitting in that chair watching you and the Australian argue."

Alison's head draws back, her mouth pursing. I've just dropped her future business in her lap, unasked for.

"Gooch…" Jerry starts.

"Three hours from now she's going to be back out in the street without a clue who I am, or you!" Alison says. "Gooch, do you not understand you just broke the Sixth Law?"

The Sixth Law says that time travel must not be known until it is known. We have ways of cleaning up after accidents that reveal it early.

"No, I did not." My voice, from the hall. My future self is standing there, in the same outfit I'm wearing, with María. María looks…different. She has changed into a white tank-top, relaxed jeans, and a last-season's red half-sleeve work shirt, the stamp of Goodwill all over her. She is still not in makeup, but has brushed and combed her hair, washed her face, brushed her teeth.

The shock on her face takes something away from her cleaned-up appearance.

"Gabriel…did you see…" She asks me, her Catalan accent thick as my morning coffee. She is unconcerned with the *joven*, the younger Gabriel Caballero standing in front of her.

I feel my brows knit. She calls me by my given name? No one calls me by my given name, except Rachel, Amá, and the tax man. *Other Mexicans* don't call me by my given name.

My *viejo* looks at her with the same knitted brows. Things are not going according to plan.

"See what?"

"See *time*…" She whispers. She has the faraway look our resident spiritualist, Erin, gets sometimes. I would not have expected a mystic out of María. My *viejo* and I both reach for her. She retreats into the darkness of the hall, screwing her eyes shut and drawing her thin shoulders up.

"Gooch, we have a *serious problem here.*" Alison says. I barely hear her.

María's thin shoulders bump against the bathroom door. Her head shoots up, her eyes go wide, looking like lanterns from the shadows. I and my *viejo* are the only ones who can see her. It dawns on me. She remembers the thump, while she was in the shower, and now she knows what caused it. A prophecy fulfilled, a predestination loop completed.

She is one of us, after all.

"Gooch!"

I meet my *viejo's* eyes. He winks at me. So this is all how he remembers it...*bueno*. He retreats into the hall after María. I turn back to Alison and Jerry. Jerry is still watching, keeping his cards close to his leather vest. Alison is on the warpath, eyes blazing under white, seer hair.

There are two polite flashes as our *viejos* disappear elsewhen.

"She just completed a loop," I comment, "bumping into the bathroom door. I saw it. She remembers."

"That's no insurance against the Sixth Law." Alison notes. "She could have been a drag-along."

I am about to mention that I just saw two flashes as two separate time-actives left the building, but I am interrupted by a welcome voice.

"No Laws of Time have been broken today." Will says, stepping into the foyer from the hall. Under the incandescent lamp, he looks like a splendid blond angel.

Where did he just come from?

"Hey, all, can't stay. The young lady in the shower is indeed ...time-active. I'm afraid further information is classified, but Gooch here's in the clear. Alison, we have a cleanup job, last night, 4:30AM and seventeen seconds. Two mundanes sighted a twinning, do you have a moment?"

Alison looks from me to Will, several times, then sighs through her nose. Alison may get hot under the collar about the Sixth Law, it being her concern and her responsibility among us, but she'll defer to the word of the Temporal Security Bureau. Especially one she's worked with for years.

"Thank you, Detective Sergeant." She says, unpursing her lips. "Yes, I can spare the time."

Will nods to each of us, a tired smile playing on his face. He looks like he hasn't slept in years. "Jerry. Gooch."

He and Alison disappear into time. Jerry sits back down on the couch, and gestures for me to sit in the overstuffed easy-chair at the back of the room.

"Now we're alone, got some business with you." He says. "This one's a freebie. I heard down the pipe something you oughta know."

I lean forward, chin on my hands, listening.

"It's about Rachel." He rumbles.

"What about her?"

"Word is she kills a time-active." He says. "Surprises him, and chokes him to death with a scarf."

IV

April 18, 2014 – 11:18:29 AM

Jerry's words are still with me when I skip back to eleven that morning. So, it's confirmed. It's known. My wife, who hates guns and cannot even butcher a chicken, kills a man with her scarf. Not just any man, a time-active man, who laughs at *la Llorna* because that old woman is so slow.

I look to Jerry, who just looks back at me with confusion. He does not know what the other Jerry said, when I have come from. So that Jerry was *mas viejo*. He does not yet know that Rachel does the horrific and impossible.

Honestly? I am a little impressed, along with everything else.

María, Jerry, *el Australiano*, and Alison are all where I left them. I look over María's dress, and wish I knew something of twentieth century women's fashion…dating her dress could be a clue itself. She mistakes my intentions, and meets my eye with a hard expression. I turn away, feeling heat rise to my cheeks.

Alison and I nod to one another: We've left that morning behind. Water under the bridge.

"Alison, do you know the style of María's dress?" I ask, very clearly. She blinks a little at me. I can feel María's softening toward me as she realizes I was not looking at her that way.

"Late 1950s," she says. "There's no waist. It's a sack-dress cut, and that came after Audrey Hepburn's collaboration with Givenchy in 1957, but there's none of the geometrical patterning that came in 1960 and after. So between 1957 and 1959."

Part of what makes my job *muy difícil* is that every time-active must be a little bit detective. And a little bit criminal. I look at the card in my shirt pocket: 1958. *Es bueno.*

"Any other questions?" asks the little Australian.

I replace the card and dredge up my interview plan from this morning, the one dashed to pieces against the Spaniard's coming.

"None of you happened to have left a note on Will's doorstep last night, have you?" I ask. Heads shake across the room. The Australian's answer is curt, Jerry' mass of hair quivers while his cheeks move, Alison stares straight at me and twitches her head back and forth. "If someone would tell Jessica Huang I would like to talk to her, I would appreciate it."

I turn to María, who is still watching…waiting.

"*Señorita* Ortega," I say in Spanish, "did you enjoy your breakfast?"

She smiles.

"Yes, *Señor* Caballero," she replies, her voice careful, guarded, "but if you are proposing lunch, I must say I'm not interested in-"

"Do not be concerned," I cut her off, "it's only a business lunch. And then a visit to the shops to get you some clothes for this millennium."

She seems openly shocked.

"But I have no money!"

I wave it off. "*De nada,*" I tell her. I am an old softie.

She rises and takes her jacket. Alison's goodbye is friendly, but perfunctory. *El Australiano* nods to me, as if I will see him again very soon. Jerry's "goodbye, Gooch," is heartfelt, and accented with a squeeze of his massive hand. He knows I will not see him again.

"So…" I begin, *en español*, "when were you born?"

"1919." She says. "I do not know my birthday."

I take a bite of my Lamb Marco Polo. The wonderful thing about San Luis Obispo is that there are four restaurants or so for every person living here, from taco trucks (with real *¡cocineros mexicanos!*) to Caffe Roma's upscale, old-family Italian by the railroad. We are sitting in a forgotten corner booth of a forgotten Chinese restaurant in a forgotten corner of a distant part of the new developments of San Luis. It is a pity, as their food is very good, but it is perfect for my purposes. They are even willing to overlook María's dress with a little bit of convincing from me. The lunch crowd is subdued, and almost entirely *gringos* and *chinos*. If anyone speaks Spanish, they are going to be very confused. Fortunately, I do not think anyone here does. The less we're understood, the better.

"I was also born in 1919," I tell her, "you were born in Barcelona, I assume?"

She nods, taking a bite of her fried rice. She munches with her mouth open, unspeaking even after she has swallowed. She is quiet, this one. I will need to draw her out.

"You were very different between this morning and when we introduced ourselves." I tell her. "I assume the others explained a few things in between?"

"Not so much," she confesses. "They treated me as their poor Catalan cousin. Family honor demands you take her in, but nothing demands that you like her."

"That is sad. They are decent people. Did they at least tell you what happened when I brought your breakfast?"

"No."

"I went..." The waitress brings our tea. She is a *gringa* but suddenly I feel cautious. "...I went down to the café downstairs. And then I came back up."

"In a moment." She says.

"Not for me." I grin. "For me, it took about five or ten minutes."

"Still not very long."

"You would be surprised how much can change in five or ten minutes." Or in a moment.

"You look at time differently from most people." María gives me a sardonic smile while I pour her tea, the way Auntie Jessica taught me. "And they all do, too."

"*Sí.*" I say. "We are a society unto ourselves. We have our own traditions, like Active Service where you help your time-active brothers and sisters. Our own language, like *viejo* and *joven*. Our own economy, which is favors and knowledge and influence. Our own laws and our own police to enforce them."

"You have a government?" She asks, disdain dripping from her voice.

"Of sorts. There are twelve ranks, from the newest raw recruit to the black-eyed powers that be, and then there is the Legion."

Something in her jumps at the mention of the Legion. I realize my mistake.

"Not the ones you are thinking of. Not the Falangists." I assure her. "They're ... well, they *are* time. They live in it. They can see it. They protect it when we can't. And after rank twelve, you join them."

"Who elects them?" She asks. "Or are they lords and kings of time?"

"The First Law of Time is *que será, será*." I explain. "If it is known that someone moves up a rank, or joins the Legion, well, that is how it happens. Especially if it's you, and *you* are the one who knows."

"And if it is known someone dies?"

I don't let her see how much that innocent question has hurt. I sip my tea instead, and try a new tack.

"How old are you?" I ask. For a time-active, this is not a simple question. My baby sister is ninety-three, and Rachel believes me when I say I am twenty-nine, but my records tell me I am thirty-eight years, three months, and eight days old.

"I don't know," she says. "I looked at myself in the mirror..."

And saw something very painful. She has led a hard life, and does not confess to pain easily. Her listener could take that knife and slip it between her ribs later.

"...and saw a beautiful woman." I help her along. She smiles into her tea, and a breath of laughter escapes her nostrils.

"An *old* woman." She tells me. "How old am I? When I last remember, I'm 17. When I look in the mirror, I look old. I know I am older than 30, because everyone over 30 looks old when you are 17."

She tightens up, her elbows drawn in, her teacup hovering near her face as if to ward me off. I reach out one hand, and she draws even farther in. I pull my hand back, and lay both of them on the table in front of me.

"*Lo siento, María.*" I apologize. "I'm sorry. This is very confusing for you."

"Mostly it's the..." she waves one hand, holding the teacup steady with the other, "...the *riches*. And the poverty. There are homeless people, and dangerous people, and desperate people. But...in Barcelona, I have seen the lines of hunger the capitalist *bourgeoisie* stamp on the women and children. Even the whores and the homeless are well-fed here. Even the whores and the homeless have cars! There is so much plenty here."

She sets the teacup down while she talks, her hands moving on their own, illustrating her rich, full, old-world Spanish.

When we left Linnaea's, she'd asked where she could get a decent cigarillo. I took her around the corner to the tobacco shop that oppresses the nose with the smell of chocolate, guarded by its *muy americano* wooden Indian. Her eyes lit up like a little boy at the candy store, but she settled for rolling papers and an inexpensive brand of Mexican pipe tobacco.

Now, she casually pulls out the pouch of pipe tobacco and sets it on the table, her fingers working automatically. With practiced hands, she shakes the tobacco into a brown paper curved to catch it. Her movements are expert, spare, without waste or haste. The measured quantity of the tan flakes, the slight depression in the middle, the pinch, the smooth-down...all this is second nature to her; it's like breathing. She holds it away from her, between thumb and forefinger, and flicks her eyes at me in search of a match.

I glance to the waitress standing behind her. The look on her face is priceless. She is staring at the beautiful handmade cigarillo as if it is a mix of space alien, cockroach, and ancient Chinese demon.

"More tea, please," María says, switching to English.

"If you are going to smoke," the woman says, her voice dripping disbelief, "please do so outside."

María looks at her with equal disbelief, and I have a feeling this can end badly. I move to rise, shuffling, making a little more noise than I need.

"Please excuse us." I say, in English. "We will be back."

I light María up outside. I don't smoke myself, but sometimes a man needs to light something on fire, so I carry a nice Zippo my Auntie Jessica gave me. The morning fog has burned off, and the sky is a beautiful blue with blown bits of white fluff like cotton floating around the floor. She turns the burning end inward and sucks it, keeping the cherry low when she takes it out. The smoke escapes through her nostrils. Now I know what she was, in 1936. That is how soldiers smoke.

The tobacco smooths her nerves. I watch her square her shoulders, loosen her mouth. We listen to children playing in the development next door, not looking at each other. We stand like *compañeros* during a *descanso para fumar*.

"Where did you learn English?" I ask, returning to Spanish. She shakes her head.

"It's very strange." She gestures at her head with her free hand. "If I think about English? I cannot remember words. I cannot speak it. But if I think about the ideas, and you speak to me in English, I can answer. Plato perhaps had the idea, when he wanted us to focus on the ideal forms and not their Earthly counterparts..."

She blinks.

"...*how do I know that?*" She demands. I shrug.

"I don't know," I tell her. "But I will find out. It is my job. You are my client."

She nods, and shifts onto one leg. No *sub-comandante* is going to come and smack her into attention. Quietly, smoothly, I click the record function on my smartphone.

"You said you woke up near running water," I suggest. Now, now the interview begins. "Do you remember where it was?"

"From here? No. But I think I can navigate from your safe-house." She says. "I think I am very good at navigating."

"What happened after you woke?"

"The Devil himself was trying to open my head with a chisel." She taps the back of her head with two fingers. She lets out a string of curses and kills any doubt about her nationality or profession. "It was painful. All I knew in the world was a painful head and fear and the cold and the dark. And the sound of running water."

She takes another drag off her cigarette. My fingers are starting to itch.

"I crawled forward, toward the sound, and wound up with my arms and face in the water," she shivers, remembering the chill. "That woke me up. Some of my memory started to come back. My name. Mama and Papa."

She turns to me, looking at me again. Her eyes run over me. I cannot mistake the look for anything, like she did with me before. Her eyes are cold, appraising, working on one and only one question:

Will this man kill me?

She decides, taking a long drag as she does.

"…and Francisco." Expressions flicker all over her face. "It was good to remember sunlight, and freedom, and the Cause."

Y el amor. She does not have to say it out loud. It is so loud it threatens to deafen me.

"I thought there was a bomb," She said. "I thought, perhaps the fascists blew a building, and I was too close?"

She takes another drag, huffs smoke from her nostrils.

"Fucking bomb-throwing statists." She says, spitting. Her voice is hard, sharp, and cold. This woman *hates*. "My eyes began to adjust, and I could see a square of faint, orange light on either side. I sat up, and the Devil did not drive his nails any deeper into my skull. I had my knives in their sheathes, and a matchbook and a card in my pocket. But it was too dark to read still. When I could stand, I did. I stepped around my little island, felt the water with my toe. That's when I ruined the toe of my shoe."

I had noted that one of her shoe toes was stained. Dirty water does that.

"I sat back down, and took my shoes and knife off, and waded through the water," she said. "When I came out, I looked up, and saw a sky that was all orange and purple. I thought, *Madre de Diós* it's starting! Franco is shelling us! But there were no artillery booms. And I could not smell the gunpowder or the fires or the burning meat."

The burning meat and the acrid gunshot smell. That's a smell you never forget…no matter how much tequila you drink. Believe me, I have tried.

"The walls were sheer, going up two, three stories, ending at that square of orange sky." She said. "I knew then I was in a drain or a water culvert or something."

She takes a last drag of the cigarette, cherry in.

"I went under two more buildings," she says curtly, flicking the butt away. "In one of them were a bunch of *ingléses* around a fire. I asked them where the *británico* camp is, I must report in, but they could not speak Spanish."

"*¿Británico?*" I ask.

"*El batallón británico,*" she replies, "the English volunteers for the struggle against the fascists and Franco. There was a camp of them stationed in Barcelona. Let's go in, my food is growing cold."

We step back inside, and I nod to the waitress as we pass. She mouths "thank you" to me. We sit down, and I pour María another cup of tea.

"Most people, they cannot remember details as well as you. You came out of the culvert after you talked with the *gring-* the *ingléses?*" I ask, while she chews a bite of rice.

She looks at me, her eyes narrowing, the crow's feet that the war stamped on her face deepening.

"Yes, I came out," she says.

"When did you realize this was not Barcelona?"

"There was a footbridge," she said, "and wide stairways and gardens and *lights everywhere*. This city is crazy, they act as if no one had ever dropped bombs on any cities in the world."

The Deep Dark. She emerged from the Deep Dark. *Ay yai yai* what a wake-up! She runs her finger along the edge of her Chinese teacup.

"I climbed up the staircase, and I saw a long white church on one side, lit up with electric lights the color of Seville oranges."

"Mission San Luis Obispo," I say. She nods along, as if to say 'whatever you say.'

"On the other side of the river, other side of the bridge, were a line of buildings with a few lights, and no people."

That will be the back side of the Higuera strip, some of the most expensive commercial land in the county. The walkways by the river and the Mission ensure a steady stream of foot traffic, and most of the bars and restaurants open back lots onto the walkway.

No people? On a Thursday night? It must have been very late…or very early. It depends on how you think about time, I suppose.

"I saw lights in a restaurant, up the street, and started walking to it. There was a flash…"

Her brow furrows, and she runs a finger along her Chinese teacup. Her hands work without her, scooping fried rice into her mouth with her spoon. She is contemplative, letting her body feed while her brain works. I do not interrupt.

"There were many flashes," she says. "It was confusing. And painful. Someone was beating me, but when I reached for my knife it was not there, and by the time I found my other knife he was gone, on the other side."

I cannot help it. My chopsticks hit the glass table top, tumble to the floor.

"Let me get you another set!" The waitress calls in English, walking away.

Free Will. The anarchist madmen who have no respect for the Laws of Time, or cause and effect, or other time-actives, or each other. Only the Free Will would attack a lost time-active in the middle of the night like that. They were trying to kill her, dancing in and out of time to do the job. Taking these catch-as-catch-can potshots is the Free Will M.O. It would have been a whole posse if she had broken the Laws of Time, and she would not now be here to discuss it.

Madre de Diós, Diós mio, the Free Will are after María. I don't know what the anarchists want with her, but I am suddenly very assured that I have two and a half days to live. If a tangle with the Free Will is in my future, I am lucky to survive so long. I barely survive the discord they inflicted on me during my Active Service.

"There were more flashes, and I had a chance to escape," she says. "I know how. I ran back for the culvert, and said to myself 'I'll wait until morning.' I found the ashes of the campfire that the *ingléses* had left, but they were gone. The warm ashes were heaven for my cold feet. I thought: I could restart the fire. I put the logs together, and reached into my jacket. My hands had brushed something while I looked for my knife, but I was too busy to think at that time. I found a book of matches, but they would not light. I tried every one of them."

She sets her fork aside, her plate bare, and takes another sip of tea. Like a good soldier, she is a good trencherman.

"It was frustrating." Her voice is cool and without emotion. "I slept some hours, I think, until the dawn came in."

"Wet and tired, it is amazing you did not die of exposure." I say.

"I am a survivor," she tells me. "The dawn was foggy like the *mistral*, and I went out. It was still very early, maybe seven o'clock? But it was light enough for me to read the card. I thought I was in 1958! Which was still a surprise, as I last remembered 1936. There was a bakery open, and I asked them how to get to the address. They chased me out because I looked like..."

She gestured down to her dress. "You saw me this morning."

Yes, I did. And it would not be hard to imagine the fear in the *gringos'* eyes. San Luis Obispo has a hatred of homeless people I have never understood. They get better, eventually, but now...

"What should I have expected? It is the usual *bourgeois* response to the crying masses of the people," she says. "Our poverty reminds them how precarious their position is, how near the revolution is."

She turns contemplative again, sipping tea while the waitress takes away her plate.

"...perhaps not so near as we had hoped." She says. "If it is 2014...I have seen police and government, so we are not yet to the stage of true communism, of mutualism. But is Spain socialist yet? And America? America is the land of Emma Goldman, so..."

"You were chased out of the bakery…" I remind her. Better for her, I think, if she doesn't know Franco won.

"I found my way to your café and your safe-house," she says. "I think I am a good navigator, even if I am in the wrong time and country."

I run the numbers in my head. She would have spent between ten minutes and half an hour finding Linnaea's from the corner of Higuera and Nipomo, where I am certain she emerged from the creek. The bakery she mentioned is probably West End Espresso… they are good, but they are no 2Dogs. Given trouble with the language, no local help, and only the street signs and the address written on the card, I would have to agree with her – a first-rate navigator.

With excellent timing, my phone starts to buzz at my belt. It startles María, but only a little.

"What is that?" She asks. I check my phone. Ah. *That* number.

"I'm getting a phone call," I explain. I wave the smartphone in front of her. Hopefully, she does not recognize the record function. "It is something important. I will be right back. Have more tea."

When I stand, she takes my hand. Her dark eyes are not killer's eyes when she looks at me.

"*Gabriel…*" she says, "…*muchas gracias.*"

It's the first time she's used my given name. It sounds very warm on her tongue.

My phone buzzes again. I slip from her grasp, and head outside. I am standing in front of the restaurant, my back to María, looking out over the parking lot and watching the cars go by.

"*¿Hola?*" I say.

"Gooch…" Jessica Huang says. "Always a pleasure."

"Auntie Jessica," I greet, "long time no see."

About twenty years, in fact. Jessica is probably somewhere in New York right now, on her way to mysterious business in the seventeen hundreds. BC. But it's not like we can leave open discussions about time travel on the wires for the NSA. Most time-actives hate phones for this reason.

"Have you been talking to anyone about Hector lately?" That should place her pretty well in her worldline.

"Hector? Hector Descanso?" Her laugh is the tinkling of silver bells. "Oh, Gooch, that was years ago."

Even better.

"So you are, what, ten, eleven by now?" I ask.

"Honey, I'm top of the pops." I can hear her grinning. "Just a few years away from the Singularity. Believe me, Hector was *years* ago."

When I ran with her in the 2030s, Jessica Huang was a rank six, taking care of green time-actives like yours truly. She ran a safe-house in downtown New York, in every sense of the word. The safe-house was still active during and after World War III, and still under Jessica Huang's command. When I was discharged after four years of Active Service, I came back to the 2030s, and kept in touch.

"I've just heard," I say, carefully, letting her know where in my worldline I am, "he's down here, trying to surveil me. You know why?"

"You know I do," she says coquettishly. There is something in her voice. Hector and Jessica? ...*¿de verdad?* That's a useful piece of information. "And I can even tell you some of it. Hector knows who rats him out. He takes off once he got his rank-six brevets, and there's a whole great chunk of his worldline I don't know anything about. About six months."

Motive and opportunity. Hector just jumped up to suspect #3, right after Lightfoot and María. I always suspected Hector would do something to get into real trouble...and now I am regretting vouching for him when Jessica *cabaceo*'d him.

"Rats him out for what?" I ask. I genuinely don't know. Unless I find out in the next few days, this will make Hector's life very complicated. Discordantly so.

In the parking lot, a Prius goes by.

"He wouldn't tell me," Jessica says. "I only found out about the... well, one of my favorite pupils feels honor-bound to tell me what happened, after the deal goes down. We put Hector's worldline together, and that was the space we couldn't account for. Other than an appearance in Brazil, watching some scientist give a talk, he's missing during that period. Could be anywhen."

Her phrasing means it is me. But I know it cannot be. So, Hector knows, or believes, I am the one who goes to Will and Park with something about him. And he has come to ...prevent it? No, whatever Hector is up to, he is not a Free Will terrorist. So...

"Have I already ratted him out?" I ask. If he is not here to prevent, he is here to punish.

Jessica's silence is all the answer she will give to that question.

"Thank you, Auntie." I tell her, after the silence becomes intolerable. "When next you are coming through, please come to dinner."

"Thank you, Gooch." Jessica says. "I think I will. Warn Rachel I'm coming."

We say our goodbyes, and I step back inside.

"What was that?" María asks.

"My other case," I say. "Almost as important as yours."

While we finish the pot of tea, I summarize her story, and wrap up the formal interview. I call for the bill, and make reassuring noises, but I do not think she needs them. Appreciates them, yes, but she long ago gave up any need for reassurance from anyone. First, we visit the corner of Higuera and Nipomo, and she and I wade through the creek into the Deep Dark until she is certain of the sites where she was attacked, where she met the homeless people, and where she first appeared. From her descriptions, I know my first guess is right...she is targeted by one or two Free Will *cabrónes*. I keep my eyes scanning close to the ground, but do not see what I am looking for. Then, I take her to Ross and to Goodwill, turning her story over in my head while she gogs at the multiplicity of choice.

How did the *ingléses* clear out so quickly? She claims she came up out of the creek, was attacked by the Free Will, and ran back into the darkness of the creek. The ashes were still warm from their fire. How had the fire burned down, and why did the homeless men not sleep around it, as would be natural on a chilly April night?

Why today? She appears and becomes enmeshed in my life when I discover I am about to die. And in my business, it does not pay to believe in coincidence. This young woman speaks casually of knives and has seen war; I fully believe she will kill. But with a scarf?

She's time-active. She could easily have skipped around last night, murdered me, alerted Will, and shown up on time for her appearance at West End Espresso. Perhaps that is what Jerry meant about her being "helpful" to my murder case. I make a note to corroborate her presence at West End.

She will not have the opportunity in her future. While she is changing, I phone Will, ask him to make sure she is surveilled at least until Easter morning. When I am not about, she will be on mundane camera, among crowds, or observed by one of us. There will not be a spare moment of her timeline that she could move in.

That still leaves last night...*assuming* she is telling the truth about events.

But, ahhh, there is one way to be sure...

When she emerges from the changing room, she is wearing a white tank-top, relaxed jeans, a last-season's red half-sleeve work shirt. It does make her look more attractive. Don't look at me like that. I love my wife, but I think my father was a wise man to say "it doesn't matter where you get hungry, as long as you eat dinner at home."

"María," I say, "head back in. We are going to skip."

She looks at me quizzically, but backs into the changing room. I look around, make sure no one is looking, and follow after her. The curtain slides closed behind us.

It is very close, in that changing room.

"María, I don't know if anyone has told you, but you are time-active." I tell her.

"I can travel through time?!" Her voice is bright and clear, unwearied by war and loss.

"Shh. Not so loud." I tell her. "The Sixth Law of Time says it must not be known until it is known, and that is in 2112. Believe me, the people outside are probably very nice people, and I do not want them to get a visit from the Temporal Security Bureau."

She goes wide-eyed, draws a line across her throat.

I shake my head, no. Well, most of the time no. Sometimes…

I feel a stab of pain for Rachel.

"I know you are time-active because I have seen you skipping." I tell her. "And the First Law of Time is that cause must lead to effect. *Que será, será.*"

"What will be, will be, hmm?" She says, rolling it around in her mouth like a good cigar.

"*Si*. It is like when I skipped to get your breakfast. Anna told me, and you told me, that I met you that morning. You told me it was interesting. So, for you to say so, I must go and meet you. And be interesting."

"A free man *must* do nothing. You must go according to who?" She asks, looking suspicious.

"According to the First Law." I tell her. "And my conscience. If I do not, it hurts you, Anna, and Uncle Jerry. I do not want to do this."

"How many of these Laws do you have?" She is persistent, I think.

"Twelve," I say. "But the only ones important to us right now are the First, Second and Sixth. Shit happens, clean your ass up, and keep quiet."

She gives me a hard eyes. She will play along, for now. But later, I need to teach this girl a thing or two about being a good steward of time.

"I have seen you in the café," I check my watch, "eight hours and forty-five minutes ago exactly. You wear this. And I come with you. Do you remember when someone bumped the door, while you were in the shower?"

She nods.

"I want you to think about that, and breathe…" I say, before switching into English. "It's like English. Do not think about how you are going to skip, just think about whenabouts you are going."

She takes a deep breath, and disappears in a flash of light. She does not blink.

I blink, and arrive next to her, in the hall of the café. María is disturbed, the others angry, my *joven* is confused. Everything is as it should be.

"Gabriel…did you see…" She did not blink.

I feel my brow furrow. Everyone blinks. It's … everyone blinks. When they skip. Everyone. But never mind, I must get back on track.

"See what?" I ask her.

"See *time*…" she whispers.

My *joven* and I both reach for her. She retreats into the darkness of the hall, screwing her eyes shut and drawing her thin shoulders up.

"Gooch, we have a *serious problem here*," Alison says, her eyes blazing at my younger self.

María bumps the bathroom door. I watch it dawn on her where the bump came from. Right now, a younger María is turning in the shower and wondering what that was. I and my *joven* are the only ones who can see. She remembers the thump, while she was in the shower, and now she knows what caused it. A prophecy fulfilled, a predestination loop completed.

She is one of us, after all. And she did not know that before.

"Gooch!"

I meet my younger self's eyes, and wink. The worry clears from my handsome young face. He looks relieved, and turns to deal with Alison. Taking María by the hand, I retreat back into the hall. Will appears next to us, the first flash I saw in the darkened hall. We nod to one another. Will looks tired, damned tired. The green eyes are rimmed with blood and dogged with shadows. The sandy hair is even greyer, though I cannot say how. And the seams of his face are drawn deeper. He looks up at me as if he has seen a ghost, or a djin.

María and I vanish together, and reappear in the Goodwill changing room. That was the second flash. Ahhhh, so that's how it happens. I had wondered how there were three time-actives but only two flashes.

María's expression is old, unhappy, and far-off.

"First time?" I ask her. She nods, too stunned to do much else. "You are lucky. Most of us do not get two first times."

She is shivering. I remember my first time. I shivered, too...

…but not that long. What did she see the rest of us don't see? I put my arm around her shoulders…I am the rock, the detective, the one piece of floating wood in a wide sea of emotion. It is a good feeling, to be the rock. She doesn't resist, and I realize we are very alone in the changing room.

Respira, Gabriel. Stay detached. You get too involved, you lose your balance. You fall. And *ay carumba* it is a long way down.

But her trembling slows down and stops.

"How do you handle it?" She asks at last. "How can you stand…what we saw?"

"I close my eyes." And I know no one else who doesn't. Not even green time-actives on their first trips or in Active Service. No one else forgets to close their eyes. No one. If she can't remember to close her eyes…she is *loca como el locote*, all messed up in her head, a lot worse than I thought.

One last shiver, casting off the pall of fear. Then, she is back to being a soldier.

"I'm sure I must have learned all this…" she says. "…once. But there is so much to learn again."

I let her go. Or she slips from me. Choose the one you like.

"Let's go out." I say. "I think they think we're a couple of teenagers. I will go out first. Follow in a minute or two."

Her smile is wan and tired, but she's trying. She makes no sound. I step outside, and find busyness in the men's clothing. While I am waiting for María to emerge, a man in a light blue shirt strides up and starts examining jeans beside me. He is wearing slacks that cost more than the entire rack of men's jeans.

He has cheekbones you can cut yourself on, and grey, grey eyes.

"Hello, Morgan." I say. He nods at me.

"A time's been set," he comments, thumbing a pair of 30-30s. "We know she's at home on Easter Sunday at 6:55 in the morning, sighted in the bedroom by a passing bicyclist. Word is already out to assemble a posse."

And with that, Morgan departs. He does not sound bloodthirsty, this time. He sounds sad.

V

April 18, 2014 – 3:20:29 AM

"Who was he, Gabriel?" María asks me, later, in the car. "What did he say to you?"

"He's a friend," I say. "It's about my other case."

She blows her smoke out the window.

"*¿No bueno?*" She asks. She already knows the answer.

"*No bueno.*" I tell her.

We drive on in silence for a while, while I deliberate. I know María did not skip last night, unless she is a very talented actress. I will surveil her movements to make sure. She definitely does not skip any time between now and Easter morning, unless Officer Matthew Park and Detective Sergeant William Howe and I all develop a sudden case of gross incompetence…which I do not think is likely. Although, we are entering a nexus, and maybe…but, even so, I am her *patrón*, she is my client, she has no motive. I have only my hunch that when time-actives are involved there are no coincidences.

If it is her, this can be one way to fox her out.

"*Muy no bueno.*" I elaborate. I outline for her the facts of the case: My body, the mysterious informant, Will and Morgan and Park, their suspicions of Rachel, Hector Descanso, Hank Lightfoot. I leave out the parts involving her, and Will's surveil of her, and what I am going to do later.

It's good to outline the case like this. I can get a feel for how things are, where they lay, who the people are.

"I think your wife and you must not be very happy if the, *como si dice*, Time Cops think she kills you." She says.

"No," I say automatically, "we are happy."

Aren't we?

We arrive at the hotel where María will stay for the night, and I idle on the street. I like them because they don't ask questions and because I can bug a room there very easily. The bug is resting in my briefcase right now: a flying bug about the size of mosquito, a lovely little souvenir from 2036. Officer Park has given me an earful about it before, but I think one or two more uses out of it won't hurt. Will or Park can collect the tapes in the morning, before the maid is in, and from there we can ensure she has a tail if she ever goes out.

Speaking of, I mentally shuffle my to-do list. I need to stake out Will's house, but I should rendezvous with Park...I can do that first. And the call of home and Rachel's arms is not to be denied. Not for long. While I am thinking, María looks out the window, and comes to her own decision.

"No," she says, flicking her cigarillo butt out the window. "No, Gabriel, I am coming with you."

Our eyes meet, and I have a metal taste in my throat.

"You are doing so much to help me, and for only a promise from Uncle Jerry," she says, steel sliding into her voice like another round into the chamber. "I do not know how much dollars are in *pesetas*, but clothing this fine cannot come cheap. Or a lunch with that much meat in it. You are a decent man, Gabriel. I will not let any *hijos de puta* kill you. We will find out who did it..."

Her jaw sets.

"...and I will stick him and let him die in a pool of his own blood." From another woman, it would be bluster, a woman's *machismo*. From María Ortega y Carrera, it is a statement of fact: *Que será, será.*

But it cannot be '*que será, será.*'

"María..." I start. Where do I start? "...*gracias* for your strong feeling. I do not doubt you can take care of my murderer."

What a woman to have on a posse! ...who needs a posse when you have the woman?

"But you cannot do this thing," I sigh. "I know I die on that beach. I have seen the body and so have others. I must die, then and there."

"No." Her word is firm and clear, a command. "There is no reason why-"

"*¡María!*" I snap. "We cannot change history. And when we have seen it, when it is part of our experience, it is *our own* history and we cannot change it."

"Why not?"

"You do not remember what discord feels like." I tell her. "It's the feeling of the universe ripping apart, slowly. It feels like you cannot breathe, cannot touch, cannot ever again be with the ones you love."

It is so much worse than that. It starts with a little memory problem, and the pounding head, and the blood at your nose, and it moves up through the exhaustion from fighting with the world, the confusion as your worldline comes apart, the struggle to hold oxygen in your dissipating lungs, until you are a delirious ghost gasping for breath with only a few frayed threads tethering you to consensus reality. And, always, you try to skip...and then you never come back.

Sometimes, I shoot the man before the posse gets too far. It is better for him.

"Like death," she comments drily.

"Yes, like *la Llorna*." I say. "And it is what happens if you try to change history. *Try*. Me, Alison, Will, Park, Morgan...even Hector and Lightfoot...when something changes, we fix it. Even if you stick him and leave him in a pool of his own blood, they will come, and give him medicine from the 2100s, so he will live again."

"He will not." she says with finality.

"Then it wasn't the right man, and they will give you a puppet to stick." I tell her. "We have ways. I have done this myself. My friends will save the man, so he can come and kill me."

"I have had friends like that." María sneers. "In Barcelona, during the war. I called them democrats."

Spoken like a true anarchist.

"Because they know," I continue, as if I hadn't heard, "because I know, that keeping cause and effect going is more important than one life."

She stares hard into me, a look I can feel congealing in my gut.

"Not even the Church has such martyrs," she says.

"Not even the Cause."

That stings her. For a minute, I think she is going to punch me.

"I told your friends and I tell you," she says, before switching to English to be sure I know she means it, "just because you can play with time does not mean you are God."

"Neither are you," I point out. "But you are deciding who lives and who dies anyway, no?"

She sighs. I have worked a crack in her armor.

"Also, if you leave him to die, he will skip away to someplace with friends and medical care. Because when he survives, he will tell them to be there with bandages and iodine." I explain. "We have a saying, 'anything that does not kill me has already been retroactively aborted.' If you are going to kill a time-active, it must be instant or nearly. He cannot see it coming."

"Gunshot?"

"Sometimes. Hit the head, neck, or heart. Heart especially. Anything that interferes with the heart makes skipping very dangerous."

"Throat slit." She suggests. "Or push the knife through. Not instant, but I do not think it will be fixed."

I am impressed and slightly worried at how this woman's mind works.

"Better to take the head off." I say. "This is why when time-actives fight, we mostly fight with time as a weapon."

Time and discord. A hell of a way to kill a man, but far more sure. She nods, following along. Her shoulders have relaxed, her hands are not fists any more.

"Besides, I didn't say you couldn't help me," I say. She looks at me, and smiles. "But we must be very clear with each other: I want you to help me find out who is responsible, and help Morgan punish him. I think you are a very strong woman, but I do not want you to break any of the Laws of Time over me, *¿comprende?*"

She scowls, frustrated. *A diós mío*, I know that feeling.

"*Si*," She replies. "But it is unjust."

The way she says it is like the shadow of the Inquisition. She says 'It is unjust' the way the inquisitor says 'It is blasphemy.' I nod. I didn't say she is not correct.

The Prius drives past us again. Do not ask me how I know it's the same Prius; it is a feeling in my gut. Someone is tailing us. Badly.

I make a quick decision.

"Will you help me on a stakeout?" I ask, dropping the English word into the sentence like a shot of tequila in my coffee. She furrows her brow. "We are going to watch someone's door, and see who goes in and out."

"Why do you need help for that?"

"We will be doing it for six or seven hours."

She nods.

"Standing watch." She feels for the paper and tobacco in her shirt pocket, and finds it satisfactory. "Yes, I am ready."

"Good." I tell her. "I have an errand to run first."

"Your meeting with, what was his name, Matthew? Matthew Park?"

"*Si*." I say, shifting the truck into gear. "Don't worry. I will be right back."

She smirks at me, the kind of look Rachel would give me. We pull around the back of the hotel to the loading dock. When there is no one around, I close my eyes.

Legends is one of the two bars left in downtown Morro Bay by 2014. If I am in the mood to dance and whoop and holler, I go to the Fuel Dock, on the other corner. But if I want a quiet beer and a game of pool, I go to Legends. I skip into the disused bathrooms behind the bar. Getting out is easy enough, and then I walk into Legends as normal. Randy is there, practicing a new drink mix in front of rows and rows of dusty bottles.

Suddenly, I want to say, 'Fuck it, fuck the whole thing,' call Rachel, and just sit in here and drink for the next two days. Discord or no discord, it's not worth it. I can just...choose not to die, can't I? Sure. That's how Free Will get born. I'm sure some of those madmen have their reasons, too.

I am still in my thoughts when Matthew Park claps me on the shoulder.

"Gooch," he greets, sitting down. I nod, still staring off into space, as if I am seriously considering going Nuremberg. "What'll you have?"

I sigh. "Ginger ale," I tell him, "I'm on the job."

Park nods, goes to the bar, and orders two. He's building rapport with me, using all our professional techniques. I know this. I still appreciate it.

"It's no fun drinking if the other guy isn't drinking with you." He grins.

"What's the news on Lightfoot?" I ask him.

He just keeps grinning at me, like a Korean jackal. I almost want to punch him. Finally, when it's *almost* too much...

"He's gone," Park says, with a little bit of a laugh. "Found out you and the girls were still around and skipped out of California and out of this century. I have a confirm that he's in Charleston in 1888 five days after he leaves jail."

I cannot describe what I am feeling at the moment. Hot? Cold? Disappointed? Happy? It is all of these things, and none of them. I take a mechanical sip of my ginger ale.

"I am pleased to hear this." I say at last. "Are you busy now that you've figured Lightfoot out?"

"If you're fishing for a favor, Gooch, go on ahead," he says. "Whatever Will says, you're my jurisdiction. And I'm the only cop in existence who's got enough time."

"You picked me up yet?" I ask him, eyeing Randy the bartender. He is a little too close, he might overhear.

"On my way there, after a good night's sleep."

"Carry me to Liao-Mueller." I tell him. Liao-Mueller is a forensics laboratory down in Santa Barbara that opens up shop in 2028. They do the best work before World War III breaks out. And I want the best. "Take the scarf with you."

"Consider it done," he says. He clears his throat, and Officer Park slips into place. "I also have a report on María Ortega."

I nod, take a sip. "Anything interesting?"

He shakes his head. We both check that Randy is at the other end of the bar from our table.

"She's *dead* tired," he says, *sotto voce*. "She naps a bit, orders room service, spends a few minutes figuring out the TV, watches the 10 o'clock news, sleeps until about 8:00 and then goes through a new downtimer's morning dealing with the 21st century's conveniences and powers. And hot water access."

"The bug followed her into the shower?" I ask, amazed. Park clears his throat, takes his own sip of ginger ale. I find myself wondering what is on the tapes.

"Do you really suspect her?" Park asks, changing the subject. "Was it her?"

"No, I don't think so," I say. "I have checked her after she arrived, it's as she said. And I assume you also have the flyer?"

"Yeah," Park says. "Gooch, *stop* bringing those little toys down here. I had to clean a flying bug out of her room, and I know exactly when that's from. You keep this up, I might need to call a forum."

"Do you have the flyer?" I ask again, meeting his eye. Officer Park's dark eyes look back at me. I feel my eyes grow cold and tired as I hold them in place. Officer Park's eyes soften into Matthew Park's. With a frustrated growl, he reaches into his coat and slaps a manila folder in my hand.

"That's because I know you won't use it again," he mutters. I mentally file to use the bug in my truck, not this one, for good temporal hygiene. "Anything else?"

Besides, I have something else in mind for the *viejo* bug. I can leave it on the beach on Saturday night. I can't look at the tapes, I would be trapped into the events they show. But someone *else* could watch them, and tell me what I need to know to make my choices.

"*Sí*, one thing," I say. "Who checks the flyer on the beach on Sunday morning?"

Park rolls his eyes, and says, "I will." I have just trapped him into accepting the inevitability of me reusing the flyer. "Don't *ever* do that to me again."

"You must admit, it is not every day a man dies," I say. He gives me an odd look, lays a hand on my shoulder, and gives me a manly squeeze.

"When did you want to meet up about the..." Some honcho passes by on his way to the bathroom. "...thing?"

"Sometime safe," I say. "Let's say tomorrow morning, Tidelands, 11:30."

"You're busy at 11:30. Noon?"

"Done."

"Anything else, guys?" Randy calls, noting the levels of our ginger ales.

"No thanks, Randy," Officer Park says, smiling congenially, "actually, could we settle up?"

While Randy's cashing out, Park turns back to me.

"Oh, don't forget the feta," he says, collecting his change. "See you tomorrow, Gooch."

I ask what he means, but he doesn't seem to hear. He just walks out the door, straight past Will. Will walks in like a man under a weight, hung from his eyes, chin, and shoulders.

"Hard day?" I ask. He sits, waves Randy off. Randy knows better than to approach Will and me together until we are good and ready.

"Could ask you the same question." We both offer a dry cough in lieu of a laugh.

In his eyes, I see myself. He is sitting close enough that I can see my face, but more than that…he knows what I am thinking, about going Nuremberg, about turning my back on the Twelve Laws of Time and doing exactly as I please and damn the timeline. Because he is thinking the same.

"Hard to stare down the barrel of your own mortality," he says, almost spitting out the words. "I'd want to run, if I were you."

I don't interrupt. Best to let the man talk, when he's like this.

He snaps his hand over my wrist. It makes me jolt.

"You can't run, Gooch," he hisses. "Please. None of us can run."

I take my hand back.

"What's wrong with you?" I ask him. "Nobody's running. I won't go Nuremburg. You know me better than that."

"It's just…seeing where you go…I don't want to see you…" he shrugs, his sandy hair quivering as his shoulders heave. "…*que será, será.*"

I raise my empty glass.

"What will be, will be." It is not a toast.

We sit in silence for a minute. It is a very long minute, and not in the way that we would sit on long stakeouts.

"I'm heading out to stake out your place." I say, more to have something to say than anything. "When you get your visitor. It's just to see who it was. Don't worry about it, but don't come out to say hello either."

He nods. As I rise, I feel the envelope. "Oh, Matthew Park is giving me hell for using a flyer on the beach. File the paperwork for me?"

Will looks up at me, as if he's never seen me before. Then, "Sure thing, Gooch. …Good luck."

I step out of Legends, into the bracing night air. Not long after, I am in another time and another place.

"Find out anything useful?" I have missed by a few minutes. María is calmly smoking another cigarillo, and wasn't when I left. Damned nexus. It's nice to hear that old world Spanish again, though.

"*Sí*," I say, "I think so. I will tell you on the way to Will's house."

I shift the truck in gear, and as one, we blink. We emerge in the same place, at eleven at night on Thursday. I chose to show up five hours early for two reasons: First, because Will might have had his time wrong, clock-bugs or no clock-bugs, and second, most of the restaurants in San Luis Obispo are still open, and we will be hungry before we are through.

We stop at the Pita Pit on the way out of town, and pick up cold pitas and Cokes. I have never needed to take care of a woman's needs on stakeout, but I am certain my lidded, wide-mouthed bottle will serve. María does not strike me as a woman used to niceties.

Already, I am thinking of her as a *compañero*, as a comrade. Dangerous, Gabriel. Very dangerous. Stay loose, stay objective.

But Will knows I'm there, and doubtless so does Park. If there is trouble, they will show, and make sure the trouble is for the other person. It is good to have friends.

By 12:30 on Friday morning, we are in place, parked on the opposite side of Kern from Will's, where the road extends into the quiet, hilly, upscale south end of Morro Bay. The hills, and perhaps even Will's property, are where the city butts up against the golf course and the state park. Will's home is palatial, a real *hacienda* of the bad old days, with its *arcadas* and *pórticos* and wings and I am not an architect, but it is big and spacious. Will's day appearance is as a retired dot-com millionaire, who is from Northern California and therefore more acceptable to the locals than an Angelino. His appointments match the image of a shrewd businessman who is, nevertheless, used to the best.

"Your friend is *de tres pares de cojones*," María comments, a socialist sneer to her voice.

"His position among us demands it," I tell her with a bit of reproach. She has much to learn. Another rank nine, the same as Will, is a leader of the San Francisco homeless, and finding him is a matter of speaking to the street people and hoping he's at the right place in his worldline.

Besides, Will has not always known such luxury.

He told me once, over quiet whiskies in the golf course Clubhouse at Clinton's re-election, that he is actually a poor 'bombchild' from the ruins of London. He spoke of life as a Yardie enforcer for the only law in town, of wandering the ever-frozen Thames in bare feet, of the things he had to do to survive, of the little sister Rosie who did not survive. He was weeping in his fine-man's whiskey when he was done. It was the only other time, besides this morning, I saw him truly emotional, undressed, without his Englishman's frigidity. Alison does not know. Morgan does not know. Park does not know. As far as I am aware, I am the only one who knows.

"And now?" She asks.

"Now," I say, clicking the seat back, "we wait."

We watch Will's front doors through the mirrors. Only a green detective or a Pinkerton points his headlights at the suspect. The trick on a good stakeout is staying awake and alert, and I have been going for … *ay yai yai* fourteen hours all together, maybe? With all its ups and downs. Another long day. This is why Will has clock-bugs, he knows when he must sleep, when he must eat. I only have my stomach and my eyelids to tell me, when one is too light or the other is too heavy.

"So," I start, as my eyelids begin to get a little too heavy. María is smoking, the movements keeping her awake despite her exhaustion. "Do you remember your Laws of Time?"

María's confusion starts deep in her chest, and only comes out of her mouth by accident.

"The First Law of Time," I hold up one finger, "is that cause must lead to effect. *Que será, será.*"

"Don't start that again," she mutters, as if telling sand not to gather in her shoes or mosquitos not to buzz in the night.

"The Second Law of Time," I continue, holding up another finger, "is that you clean up after yourself. Sometimes you misplace something, or otherwise get hit in the head with discord. So you clean it up."

"It's really that bad?" She asks, her Catalan accent twisting even that simple question nicely.

I remember the man I killed in Active Service. I remember throwing my arms around him as he tried to skip away from me. I remember coming out the other side with his heart's blood on my hands, because his chest was no longer there.

"It's really that bad." I tell her. I sound like a *paisano*.

"But that violates the first law," María points out, waving her lit cigarillo at me. "If it's impossible to change history, why is there a rule about what to do when you change history?"

"Because it starts ripping the universe apart," I point out, "starting with you. And it means your friends have to come clean up after you. Or the Time Cops. Or worse."

"What happens if nobody cleans it up?"

"I don't want to know."

A car drives by. We both fix on it in our separate mirrors, suddenly alert. Wide-set headlights, rectangular…older car. It drives past without stopping.

"The Third Law of Time," I say, popping up a third digit, "is to call if something goes wrong, and heed the call if you hear it."

"What do you mean, call?"

"We all talk to each other," I say. "We *all* talk to each other. And if you are my *amiga*, I will find time to meet up with you and help you with your problem. It can be someone out there or it can be some *loco* time-active picking a fight with you."

Or it can be a Free Will anarchist trying to kill an innocent woman who woke up in the creek.

"Why didn't anyone show up when I got attacked last night?"

"You don't know they didn't," I point out. "You mentioned 'lots of flashes,' no? How do you know your friends did not cover your escape?"

"Why didn't they follow me?"

"You told me everything, and I think you told me the truth."

I let that rest. She just meets my gaze with steely dark eyes.

"So we know what happened, and we can't change history." Her eyes flick out the window, and her cigarette flicks into the ashtray. "Maybe I should not have told you so much," she adds.

"The Fourth Law of Time," I say, "is not to fill the universe with us."

For a good Catholic boy, it is a hell of a thing to know he can never be a father. And what will happen to his wife and child, his *familia*, if he ever tries.

She nods, jaw tight, the tendons popping out of her cheeks. She understands, I understand. She bridles to hear it, I bridle to hear it. Without thinking, we clasp hands.

"The Fifth Law of Time," and I hold up one outstretched hand, "is that you must respect yourself. You see you, you pay attention to what she's doing. And when you are her, do what she did. It's easiest to fuck up your own history when you're with yourself."

"I don't know if I'd like to meet me," she says, staring at her cigarillo thoughtfully. "I am not the nicest person."

I can't argue with her there. Rachel screws her eyes shut when she hits me in play, this woman I am sure watches her target die when she slips the knife in. Not because she enjoys it, but to *make certain*.

"Well, you never know," I say, "if you can't trust yourself, who can you trust?"

She shrugs.

"The Sixth Law of Time," I move swiftly on, holding up my other hand with one digit already up, "is that time travel must not be known until it is known. And the big reveal comes in 2112, so we're ninety-eight years early."

"Why is there such a stupid Law?" She asks. "We are time-active and most people are not as progressive as you and I. Let the people know, give them the power, so they can defend themselves! I am surprised that your friend Will did not prevent the rightful owner of that house from being born just to take it."

I consider my answer for a moment, stroking my chin.

"My wife, she is big and broad and very good with a baseball bat," I say, "*she* is the reason for the masquerade."

María laughs, the first real, full laugh I have ever heard from her…maybe the first real, full laugh anyone has ever heard from her. It starts somewhere in her gut and shakes all the way up.

"To be serious, they outnumber us by billions. I think. At least millions." I say. "If they wanted to, we could not stop them all. And they would not stop with men like Lightfoot, they would also kill you and me."

Once upon a time, they did. No one goes to Vinland, unless they go there to die. That sobers her a little. She takes another puff of her cigarette.

"The Seventh Law of Time…" I intone, holding up seven fingers.

And so the stakeout goes, laughing, smoking, eating our pitas. As I suspected, she makes as good use of the wide-mouth bottle as I do, and she has enough *caballerosidad* to look away, same as I do.

"Usually," I say around five AM, "I bring the cheap detective fictions."

"You read mysteries while you're on a stakeout." She deadpans, using the English for both 'stakeout' and 'mysteries.' It is my turn to shrug.

"They are not too interesting so I don't have to worry about not paying attention." I say. "But I admit, it is much nicer to spend the stakeout with a pretty girl."

"Your accent is cute," she says, before staring horrified at me. I chuckle. She chuckles.

"Usually it's the silly man who says such silly things," I say. She pops the cherry in her mouth. After a long smoke, she speaks again.

"I've never been very good at the whole man-woman thing," she confesses. "When I was young, I dreamed I would marry a poet, because he would forget such things when the other men didn't push his *machismo*."

Something moves in the mirror. Will's porch light is on. I slap María's shoulder lightly, to get her attention. With my chin, I gesture toward the rearview mirror. She looks to the passenger-side mirror. We both watch as a man steps out of Will's house, and closes the door behind him.

I pull out the binoculars almost as quick as I can draw the Colt, and have them to my eyes. It's early yet, and still dark enough that I can turn around without drawing attention. The set of the shoulders, the gait, the sandy blond hair…it's Will, all right. He hurries to his car, starts it, and takes off down Kern.

María and I are silent, waiting, when he returns eleven minutes and twenty seconds later. He's got a hand-carry white paper bag, looks like a Rite-Aid bag. He heads straight into the house and shuts the door behind him. It's now 5:08AM on Thursday morning. Will said his visitor came around 4:30AM, I do not remember exactly.

"Hm..." I say, "the curious incident of the visitor in the night-time."

"...There was no visitor in the night-time." María comments, with furrowed brow. I grin.

"That is what was so curious about it, my dear Ortega." *I have always wanted to say this!*

I put my truck in gear, and drive away into the afternoon just as the light is dawning.

We emerge two hours after we left, and my phone starts buzzing again.

"*¿Hola?*" I ask.

"Gabriel Caballero y Gutiérrez!" My wife screams so loud that María can hear her. "Where in Hell are you?!"

"...S-San Luis..." I say, clearing my throat and feeling the blood run from my face. *Chingao* what did I forget this time?

"Well getcher hot tan ass back to the damn house!" She shouts. "It's Thursday, Will's coming over, remember? And Will mentioned something about Jessica being in town. Why don't you *tell* me these things? Did you remember the cheese from TJ's?"

I can almost see her, *como agua para chocolate*, pulling her hair out with one hand, holding her cell with one hand, stirring the soup with

one hand, pulling out the roast with one hand, and waving off
Debbie-Anne's well-meaning 'help' with one hand. Also stamping her
foot like the house has cockroaches and turning almost as red as her
sofrito.

This must be what Park meant.

"I'm just pulling into Trader Joe's now." I lie.

Rachel sighs, or howls. I don't know how to describe it. She
makes this noise when she realizes she cannot change things and
must accept them as they are, but she does not have to like them.

"Look, just…get here by six." She clicks the phone off. I feel her
frustrated scream, all the way out in San Luis. Somewhere in Morro
Bay, she just set off car alarms.

María looks on.

"Big and strong and good with a baseball bat, yes?" She
deadpans.

"Yes." I check the time. Five thirty-five. *Pinche puto pendejo baboso.*

María yawns, and I remember where we are.

"María," I say, "it has been a long day. Get a good night's rest. I
need a good night's rest."

María wisely does not comment on whether I will get it. *Muy
inteligente.* I start the truck, and pull around to the front of the hotel.

"It has been very interesting." She says as we pull up. "Thank
you for lunch. When is the rendezvous?"

I startle, then realize she could not possibly have meant it that
way. In Mexico, 'rendezvous' means *rechinar la cama*, to make the bed
go squeak. But I am pretty sure María does not mean it this way.

I glance at her. She seems very relaxed, uncrossing the legs that seem so long on her.

Pretty sure.

"I will pick you up tomorrow morning." I tell her. I do not want to make her skip around more than she needs to. "Nine o'clock. Be checked out."

She nods. I handle her through check-in, and escort her to her room. I do not have time for this, but it must be done. While the *viejo* bug sits in my jacket pocket in its little envelope, I take the *joven* bug out of its usual spot in my briefcase. I leave it in the potted plant while she is busy with another cigarette. I will ask Park to pick up the tapes in the morning so we can back-fill our knowledge of her worldline later.

You are asking, why am I concerning myself with this? Park has already told me what is on the records. But if I do not lay the bug now, he cannot pick it up in the morning. If he does not pick it up in the morning, he cannot review the records. If he does not review the records, he cannot tell me what is on them, and the whole process comes crashing down. Park and I get smacked with discord next time we skip, even so much as a second, until someone actually leaves the bug in place. Had I left the older flying bug, from the envelope, it would be the same problem, because where does the original flyer come from then?

You would not believe how much of a time-active's life is taken up with such matters of time as this.

I check my watch. Five fifty-five. I drive around to the loading dock, but there is a truck there. *No es bueno.* Casually, as if I know what I am doing, I drive back out and towards Trader Joe's. Next to Trader Joe's is a long industrial way, ending in a dead end about three blocks up. In the dead end, I disappear to an hour and a half earlier…that should be long enough.

I get two cheeses at Trader Joe's, the feta Rachel requested and the triple-cream brie that she loves so much. I also pick up a bottle of Conundrum by way of apology, though I am sure Will and his wife are bringing a bottle to go with dinner. God only knows what Jessica is bringing.

I flinch for my phone to warn Rachel of Jessica's arrival before realizing the time. I cannot call her, or she will not mention it and I won't know to call her. *A diós mio*, I must be tired.

On the drive home, I listen to the interview I had with María at lunch. *Madre de Diós*, it feels like so long ago now!

I am glad of the extra time I gave myself. I have enough time to stop by Top Dog Café in Morro Bay and get an espresso and a public bathroom shave before I go home. I do not like to run business this way. This is how I usually like to run business: plenty of time, plenty of money, plenty of follow-up. I don't have to listen to my recordings of interviews in a café bathroom while also trying to shave.

Normally, for a case like María's, I would be systematically checking up and down Morro Bay and putting feelers out towards our Spanish *amigos* in the 1930s. I'd be checking paperwork to see when and where she maintains a residence, and under what name. I can ask Morgan to hand me a dossier when he is surveilling María's appointment at West End Espresso tomorrow morning.

I tap my razor on the restroom sink, and make a note to surveil her last night after a good laugh and a long sleep. Then she mentions the 'multiple flashes,' and I hear my chopsticks fall to the floor.

I also make a note to clean my guns and make sure they are loaded.

While she's talking, I look at the card in my pocket. Mike's Barber Shop. …they do not cut women's hair. Not in 1958. Why would she have an appointment there?

Not to mention my own case. Why is Will acting so odd? Where is Hector Descanso and why hasn't he come yet? At least I don't have to worry about Hank Lightfoot any more. That joker might be a pain in my ass, but if Officer Park's hounded Hank Lightfoot out past World War I, I can put money that I won't see him again.

Shaved, coffeed, and with a splash of water on my face, I am almost a new man. And it is almost six o'clock. After rinsing the last hairs down the drain, I step out and tip the girl generously for taking the One Last Customer, of whom Rachel has told me many times. I head out for my truck.

Time to go home. We're having a party.

VI

April 18, 2014 – 5:59:32 PM

"Lucy, I'm home!" I am extra theatrical, and our guests chuckle.

The living room is clean and tidy, which I can only assume is Debbie-Anne's work. Both Rachel and I are too fond of our knickknacks and our active lifestyles that we can't be bothered to clean. Tidy, yes, we are not savages. But usually our home is comfortably lived-in, not picture-perfect like this.

Debbie-Anne is holding court in the den area, gold curls and white pearls shining, looking *encantadora* in her new dress. The gas-fireplace is simmering on low and the house is pleasantly warm. One bottle of white wine, looks like Castoro Cellars from here, is already open and set on the coffee-table next to the nachos and salsa. Debbie-Anne is seated to one side of the fireplace, and Amá is on the other, relishing the warmth.

Will makes the perfect complement to Debbie-Anne's regal demeanor, with his severe, perfect looks. He looks much more put together now, though I do not know if he is here before or after his visit to Legends. His holster is missing, leaving a telltale worn spot on his belt. He can play the part of *nouveau riche* all he wants, he still has a worn belt where his gun sits all the same. I find myself wondering where in his worldline Will is.

I lay down my burdens and hang up my jacket and my own holsters, surreptitiously hanging Will's gun inside his jacket as well.

Ah! Beautiful domesticity, all the ordinary and everyday, it warms your heart.

My heart freezes as my glance slides over the soft cotton scarf on the next peg.

"Hun?" Rachel is still in the kitchen. I snatch up the canvas Trader Joe's bag where I laid it, and stride into the kitchen.

"Good evening, Gooch." Jessica's voice is warm and buttery.

Xirui Jessica Wu has her fine tapering arms folded, one of them raising a glass of the white wine towards her lips. The color of the wine contrasts brilliantly with the earthy color of Jessica's skin. She has the jet-black eyes of the rank twelves, a dark, glossy coif, and a curling smirk all her own. She's being daring tonight, and wearing some of the latest styles of 2036, all callbacks to the late twenty-tens but with an Asian-space sensibility. Will clearly doesn't approve, but he'll let it slide for now.

"Jessica!" I say, feigning surprise. "Long time no see. But would you excuse us a moment? I would like to speak to my wife."

She takes her sip, and raises an eyebrow at me before floating into the living room. I turn to Rachel. She's wearing a peasant shirt with long sleeves, and the same swishy skirt, and birkenstocks. Little touches and accessories here and there announce that this is her dressing nice for a friendly dinner party, and not just another night at home. She's let her hair down, and it comes down in bronze waves to the curve of her breast.

Rachel looks absolutely beautiful. And it must show in my eyes, because I can see her mouth relax, the outside of her eyes smooth out.

I feel a vision, Rachel, her scarf, my mottled face, her tears...all I want to do is take her in my arms, and hold her, and warn her that I will soon be gone and make the best of our blood in our veins and our time in our hands.

Wordlessly, because otherwise I might sound unmanly, I pull out the feta and hand it to her. She smiles. I pull out the Conundrum, and watch the wisps of flame she calls eyebrows rise up her brow. Finally, I pull out the brie she loves. I wonder if I will get to watch her eat it.

She looks at it curiously, the way she looks at one of her math puzzles, then sets it on the counter. She takes a deep breath, steadying herself for the jump.

"Gabriel," she says, her voice rich with conflicting emotion, "we have to talk."

I feel the shiver run down my spine. We are lucky everyone is around the fireplace, where they cannot see us over the breakfast counter.

"Talk?" I hiccup.

"You forgot about the dinner party, didn't you?" Rachel asks. "I'm surprised you remembered the feta."

She turns to the stove, in the deepest part of the kitchen, where dinner is just coming together. She made some kind of curry, rich and caramel-colored. That's my woman: delicious, worldly, simple, and hearty. I reach out.

"I don't know what in Hell is so important!" Her voice cracks a little on the last word. She looks like a steamer about to overheat and blow scalding water everywhere.

"Rachel, *amor mio…*"

"Your *amor*," her cackle is sharp and digs between my ribs, "you lie to me and slip out of bed in the middle of the night and I wake up and just for a moment I wonder if you're *dead* and Matthew Park's going to show up this evening with that *tell-the-missus* look on his face and you can't even find time in your busy-ass day to remember your own *wife!*"

She's turned back to me, murder in her eyes, the last word ringing the entire house. There is total silence, accented by the hiss of the gas fireplace.

I can feel the fire climbing up through my dress shirt. I have no problem with fighting, and she and I have worked out more than a little frustration in footraces or 'rasslin" as she puts it. But you do not involve guests in your household dispute. A man's house is sacred and his hospitality, moreso. I am starting to see red, and it's not Rachel's hair.

"Quiet down, woman," I growl at her, "we have friends over."

"Oh ho," she laughs, matching my quiet danger. "No, sir. *I* have friends over, Gabriel. You barely remember you *have* friends. And I will argue in front of them if I damn well please. Friends *understand* when your husband's a…when he…"

She mouths another few words, but her voice is not there. The frustration sends her over the edge. Grinding her teeth, she steps out towards the breakfast nook, where she will shout at everyone. I clasp my hand over her wrist.

"Rachel, please." I warn. "Let's just have a good time."

She snaps her wrist from my hand as if my touch were corrosive. She pants a few times, impaling me with the Evil Eye, then spins on her heel, marches to the back of the house, and slams the bathroom door.

I take a minute, bracing myself with my hands at the corners of the stove, to breathe hard and let my ears stop throbbing. No one comes in to check on me, not even Amá. I don't know if that makes them good friends or bad ones.

Finally, with a breath as hard as kerosene over the top of the burbling curry, I turn around. I try to relax my face, and smile, and I walk out into the living room.

Will is still on the couch, and Amá is still enjoying the heat of the fire, but Debbie-Anne is gone and Jessica is reclining in the chair opposite Will. Without Debbie-Anne, everything is more subdued. Even the fire seems turned down.

Will's green eyes are telling, and we have worked together long enough that I can read the whole conversation in them.

"Oh, you know," I say, hooking my thumbs in my belt, "sometimes husband and wife have a little spat. Don't worry about it."

By the fire, Amá grins.

"You fucked up," Amá comments in Spanish.

"*Muchas gracias*, Amá," I tell her sweetly, flushing in my cheeks. I am lucky no one else here speaks Spanish, but I watch Will's blond eyebrows inch up.

Jessica takes another sip of wine.

"Did you make the salsa, Gooch?" She asks lightly. "I seem to remember it tasted like this when I tutored you, back in New York."

As one, we all note Amá, meeting her blind eyes with our own. Were it not for my baby sister, we would be three time-actives alone in a room, able to converse freely. No one is foolish enough to assume she understands so little English as she pretends.

"Oh no, it was Rachel," I say. "She's the genius in the kitchen. I don't think my mother could make it as good as this. Is there any wine left?"

Jessica and I nod to one another, me in thanks and her in acceptance. I pour myself a glass, but not before topping off everyone else like a good host. The wine is soft and buttery as Jessica's voice…a very California chardonnay.

"Amá," I say, "how is your guitarwork coming?"

"I think I've gotten a hold of my *glissando*," she says.

"Would you favor us with your playing? I haven't gotten the tune you played this morning out of my head."

"Someone will have to get my guitar," she says, "unless you want to send a blind woman out into the night."

I nod to Jessica, and she disappears in a flash. On my mother's grave, I swear that woman can *skip* ostentatiously. There is a comfortable silence.

"You see Park?" Will asks.

"Made the rendezvous," I answer. He is looking intently at me, as if his green eyes could bore into my head.

"You have to tell them," he says, his words clipped, his bombchild accent thrusting to the surface. "You have to."

"What do you mean, I have to?" I demand. That intensity is gone from him, his lines less severe.

"Sorry, Gooch," he said, "I didn't mean to..."

"I know, *amigo*," I tell him, "but it is not appropriate dinner conversation."

His stare is unsettling. The silence drags, long, unnatural. It is not our comfortable silence.

"We all have our duty to do, Gooch," he says, looking away. He is reciting from a long-ago school book. "'All the world's a stage, and men and women merely players. They have their exits and their entrances, and one man in his time plays many parts.' You have to talk about it, here, tonight."

I am about to rise and demand what Will thinks he is doing, laying out my future like that, and in my own house, about to eat my own bread. Jessica's timing is impeccable.

"Here you are, Ms. Caballero." Jessica says, laying the Spanish guitar in Amá's untrembling hands. Amá warms up with a few scales, and then plays one of her favorites, "Bolero Mallorquin." I let myself get pulled away in it.

While she plays, I feel the presences of the McCoy sisters moving through the living room and into the kitchen. I know better than to turn around. Besides, Francesca's playing really is beautiful, the full rich sound of warm evenings in the plaza and the taste of tequila and the forward girls of far-gone Jalisco in their ruffles and Sunday finery.

As the last note dies away, Rachel clears her throat. We all turn to the dinner table, which has been laid with bread, butter, the

Conundrum, candles and a Greek salad with the feta. Debbie-Anne douses the lights, leaving us glowing in the firelight. On her sister's behalf, she also gives me the Evil Eye. It is amazing how much it looks the same, given that Rachel has brown eyes and Debbie-Anne, blue.

"Dinner's on!" Rachel sounds happy as a clam at high tide, laying the pot of curry on the table, the blue enamel setting off the caramel color beautifully. "Come an' git it!"

There are coos of appreciation and wonder at Rachel's table spread, and Jessica comments on the hours it must have taken. But I know better. Rachel made the salad ahead, without the olives and feta, and bought the bread fresh from work today. She already had the meat and the vegetables for the curry chopped up when she went to bed last night, and used a block of that Japanese curry mix you can get at the Oriental Market in SLO. As to the salsa, *Madre de Diós* I am a *jalisciense*, do you think I would let my wife let us go a day without good salsa? *Ay yai yai.* The whole thing took her maybe half an hour tonight.

Genius in the kitchen, no?

I lay Amá's hand in my elbow, and she sets her guitar aside. She lets me lead her to the table, pull out the chair, tuck her in. She says '*gracias*' while I pour her a bowl of curry. She feels around for the silverware with one hand, and I guide her sensitive fingers to the bread, the bowl, the candles, her salad. She nods when she knows where everything is, and takes up her spoon.

My sister is a Caballero born and bred, she will need me to pour another bowl before dinner is done. I pour myself a bowl, and get some of the salad, and seat myself at the head of the table. Rachel and Debbie-Anne are seated at the foot, and we are all fine with this. Amá is on my left hand, Will on my left, and Jessica in the middle. All have served themselves, but are waiting on me.

I bow my head.

"Pater noster," I intone, "qui es in caelis…"

I grew up before Vatican II. It's not *right* unless it's in Latin.

"…Amen."

With our grace finished, I look up at my friends and family and smile. The digging-in is marked by the coos and compliments to the chef, who looks radiant with the fire burning low behind her and casting her in the colors of sunset.

The curry is warm and full of flavor, but not too hot, the carrots are firm and the potatoes soft, and I do not know what she did to the fish, but it is tender and moist as all fish should be. The wine goes well with it; I would not think a Conundrum would stand up to all the flavor. The cool, sharp tastes of the feta, olives, vinegar and greens also set off the warm, cloying curry sauce beautifully. *Mi amor.*

I look up from my dinner, and find Will's glance there. He looks like a bronze bust of some old Roman emperor, one of the good ones, his perfect marble angles and his worn green eyes. Without words, he is asking me to do my duty. To say what Park told me, and, in a sense, to go to that beach. To obey the First Law of Time and ensure *que será, será.*

"I have news on Lightfoot," I say, setting down my spoon. I feel my chest run cold, and look to Debbie-Anne. She's paused in the middle of her spoonful of curry, her mouth trembling a little. Rachel is starting to see red at the name. She looks ready to murder me.

"He's gone." I wear my friendly grin like a too-hot mask. "As soon as he got out, he split."

"How far?" Will asks.

I meet his green eyes.

"Very. Far." I enunciate. Not in front of the others, *si, comprende*. I turn back to my wife and her sister. "According to Officer Park, he found out that you two and yours truly were still in town and he wanted to run as far as he could go."

Rachel's smile is a terrible thing to see.

"Wow," Jessica comments, "what did you three *do* to him?"

"It's not really dinner-table conversation," I say, trying to wave it off. That's all that they need to know about the rendezvous, but everyone makes insistent noises and gesture at their appetites, which will not be dulled by scary stories.

Rachel, Debbie-Anne, and I all exchange glances: nonverbal you-firsts all around. We all, as one, take a mouthful of wine. This will be a long story.

"He was my boyfriend," Debbie-Anne starts, her drawl coming out. "I met him not long after I moved to Texas. At first, he was so charming…a sweet Southern boy with a twist."

Some twist. He has a list of domestic violence accusations as long as my arm, in three centuries and seven countries. Including one in the Confederate States of America, where he hails from.

"He was tall, dark, handsome…" Debbie-Anne's voice is dangerously wistful.

"*Deborah Anne McCoy.*" This time, Rachel doesn't even have to raise her voice.

"Right. But, uh, it didn't work out." Debbie-Anne isn't sure what to feel right now. "So, back in oh-nine, I …broke it off. With him. I was living in Houston at the time, and so was he. The next week, he came to my apartment to 'talk about it.'"

Debbie-Anne's voice dries up.

"He put her in the hospital," Rachel finishes, her voice steady.

"Yeah…" Debbie-Anne confirms. Without her noticing, she flexes that left hand. She squares her eyes to the table. Even Amá looks away. Only Rachel and I meet her gaze. "I'm lucky the neighbors were so friendly. They called 9-1-1 before he got …too bad."

Debbie-Anne's left eye was swollen shut, and her lip so fat she lisped like a Spaniard, and it was only good luck the fine fluted bones of her face were not broken. Her wrist *was* broken. Somewhere in Paris in 1832, there is a half-mad French whore who will never walk. Also courtesy of Hank Lightfoot.

A lawyer friend of mine, he works with domestic violence. He says what gets him is "how depressingly predictable" every case is. He stopped thinking about work years ago. We drink together sometimes.

"While I was in the hospital, I got a visit from a very nice Mexican man." Debbie-Anne's eyes sparkle in the candlelight as she lifts her chin at me.

"*Si…*" I say. "…Lightfoot had skipped bail for, of all things, a domestic violence charge."

In 2033.

"I took the case for a friend of mine, who referred me a lot of business in those days."

Jessica meets my eyes, but only for a flickering moment.

"Hank Lightfoot, he is not good people." I say. "He has a rap sheet longer than my arm, although not so long as Rachel's arm. Domestic violence, two priors for assault, this kind of thing. All girlfriends. No convictions."

Debbie-Anne has gone quiet again.

"How did he manage to get away with it for so long?" Jessica asks, her dark coif shimmering in the candlelight.

"Men like Lightfoot have an M.O," I say. "He usually splits town when the heat gets to be too much on him. He had had trouble with the law one or two times…"

Now it's Will who meets my eye. Detective Sergeant Howe and Officer Park assisted the Paris *Sûreté* in putting the fear of God and the Temporal Security Bureau into Lightfoot when he left certain toys and knowledge loose in 1832. I will give Lightfoot credit, when he sees force of will in action, he respects it. I do not know of him ever violating the Laws of Time after that.

"…But nothing ever seemed to really stick."

Beating a woman so bad she will never walk again? Not Detective Howe's or Officer Park's jurisdiction… move along. Can't start making moral judgments, or where will it lead? The Legion declaring war on the United States for genocide, with a posse led by Crazy Horse? No no, leave mundanes their law and we will have ours.

But leaving a computer on a desk or leaving that woman's mind half-intact so she remembers who the computer belongs to? That earns a roughing-up, six months' surveil and a very stern warning.

"So when his M.O. cropped up," in 2009, "in Austin, Texas, I headed out to see what happened. The Austin police, they were very helpful."

Will's well-formed smile tells it all. "Better than these MBPD assholes." His smile says. "Better than Matthew Park."

"They pointed me to the *señorita*. He was using an assumed name, but I knew my man. I thought I could catch him then and there, but I think he had a tipoff. At the time I cursed up a storm."

I look straight into my wife's beautiful honey-brown eyes.

"Now I am glad he escaped me in Texas."

No matter how angry she is, even Rachel cannot help smiling at that. Or blushing.

"I advised this little blonde *señorita* to take a vacation for a few weeks and to take out a restraining order, because Lightfoot does not give up easily." I take a sip of wine. "Not without encouragement."

"She came to visit me." Rachel breaks in. "I was living with a friend at the time and after Debbie-Anne told me everything, nothing was too good."

"Remember what you said?" Debbie-Anne says, grinning and gesturing her spoon at Rachel. "You said if he got anywhere near me you'd smack him upside the head."

"With Dan, yeah." Rachel says smugly. They both chuckle.

'Dan' is Rachel's prize Louisville Slugger…she made the winning home run in a college game with him. She keeps him oiled and waxed by the front door, next to her scarf. It is not very funny to me.

"And *you*, you little shithead," Rachel continues, and she really does sound like her mother, "you forgot to file that restraining order in California."

"Lucky for her, I didn't," I mention. Rachel nods. "But I knew that the law might come too late, so I came to the apartment where her sister lived. I heard about this sister, how she was big and tough and very, very *loud*."

"I am not!" Rachel whines, in a drawl that fills the house.

"And also very smart." I finish.

"And when he came to the door and he saw me," Rachel says, grinning from ear to ear like the overgrown tomboy she is, "he said '*Sangre de Christo* Debbie-Anne didn't say you were also beautiful!'"

A smile breaks out over Debbie-Anne's angel face. It is good to see. She has been silent and sullen for some time.

"An' you were wearing yer overalls and that Obama t-shirt!" Debbie-Anne laughs. "Oh, lordy, your *hair* that day…"

"Shut up, sis." Rachel is trying to sound angry, but doesn't really mean it.

Rachel had been in the backyard of the house, building and painting a portable skate-park for poor kids in Santa Margarita. She was splattered with paint and covered in sweat and had a streak of white paint plastering her bangs to her brow where she'd wiped sweat off with the back of her hand and she really was absolutely beautiful.

It was the smile, the all-over smile of someone doing good work and knows it.

I hadn't seen anyone smile like *that* in a long time.

"So I asked who the hell he was," Rachel says, "and he said he was the detective from Texas. I asked him for his license number..."

"And I fell in love right then." I say, chuckling around a spoon of curry. I swallow, and continue. "She is beautiful and smart from books and she knows to ask a man's license number when he comes to the door? *Ay yai yai*, give me one of *those!*"

I left myself a 2009 detective license on the hotel room counter that morning, with a note that says "When she asks, show it to her. You will know then." I still have the note, in my stuck desk drawer.

"I invited him in and offered him sweet tea." Rachel says, although it was tea with some kind of bizarre and all-natural sugar substitute. Agave, I think. Waste of good agave. "And he told me he needed Debbie-Anne's signature for the California restraining order. She was out with my roommates, but I told him she'd be back in a few hours."

"And she took me out back to see the skate-park project for Santa Margarita she put together." I grin.

Rachel is practically glowing.

"Well, I put the blocks together..." She looks back to me, and there's a ghost of that afternoon's smile on her lips. "...and Gabriel helped."

We spent the whole afternoon with hammers and nails and paint and sunshine and laughs.

"When Debbie-Anne got home, I think she was a little surprised," I say.

"A *little* surprised, sugah?" Debbie-Anne cocks one light brown eyebrow at me. "I felt like I'd seen a ghost!"

"I got her signature, and I gave her an alarm." I feel the pall of Lightfoot's shadow come creeping back over the table. Amá's bowl is empty. I stand with an 'Excuse me,' and fill her up again. "It's standard procedure that someone at risk of a second assault, especially like this, should have a direct alarm."

Officer Park never quite forgave me for giving Debbie an alarm from the 2030s. But my phone then was not backward-compatible, so anything earlier would not have also alerted me.

"It was so small!" Debbie-Anne says. "And he explained that all I had to do was push the button if he even came to the door and he'd be looking at a year, minimum."

"There were some warning signs. A few phone calls, a sighting or two."

"That drunk-dial," Rachel mentions. Debbie-Anne shudders at the memory and takes a gulp of wine.

"And meanwhile," I continue, "Debbie-Anne has this sister..."

Is it wrong that I look back on those few weeks as some of the happiest of my life?

"You were looking out for the poor woman," Amá comments, "of course."

I translate, and all assent "Of course." There's more spooning of curry and stabbing of salad. The salad really is wonderfully tangy.

"So one night, I'm preparing dinner for three-" Rachel says.

Debbie-Anne doesn't contradict her. Wise.

"-and I've just sent Gabriel out to grab some wine to go with the risotto." Rachel's face drops at the memory. "I hear the door but I'm busy folding the rice and tell Debbie-Anne to get it."

She just stares at her sister.

"I promise I always check the peephole now," Debbie-Anne says sheepishly, squirming a little in her chair.

"That fucker starts threatening her," Rachel says, "shoving her up against the couch and telling her she has to take him back, he's got nowhere else to go. And I'm just thinking 'hit the damn button! The alarm! Hit the damn button!'"

She takes a sip of wine. We're all hanging on her word. Even Amá is leaning forward and has fixed her blind eyes on Rachel's voice.

"She says no, and he's about to really give it to her," she says. "So I tell him to get the hell out of my house."

"While waving a kitchen knife," Debbie-Anne notes.

"While waving a kitchen knife," Rachel confirms, "and while his back's turned, I reckon Debbie-Anne'll be able to hit the alarm or call 911 or something. She hightails it for the bedroom and locks herself in, and you *left the damn alarm sitting on the coffee-table!*"

"Sorry!" Debbie-Anne squeaks. "I was just, I didn't know what I was doing, what was happening..."

"I know, sugah," Rachel says, squeezing Debbie-Anne's hand. "We were both scared. Fear makes people do stupid things sometimes. So, I tell him to get out, again, and he just laughs at me. He says he's got one good chance and rushes me. I hold the knife out."

And blinked. Rachel can't stand real violence, and when we wrestle I always know when she's going to hit because she screws her eyes shut.

"…somehow he's behind me and he's got the knife at my neck." She shivers. "He tells me he's going to cut me and while he's talking I hit him with everything - I mean *everything*. Smack him with my head and hit him with the elbow and step on his instep and everything. I don't even remember."

Casually, she stretches one arm out on the table, her right, with its mottled green and purple bruises and shiny white scar. Debbie-Anne looks on with wide eyes and a greenish look.

"The only thing from 2009 is that scar…it looks worse than it was." Rachel lies, before pulling her sleeve back down. "He lets go and all I can think of is that damn alarm. I go over the couch and land half on the coffee table. He looks real bad, all dazed from where I hit him with the back of my head, and I hit the button."

The message appeared on my phone, a day and a time down to the second. That's all. I know when he is, and where he is, and that he's too close to Debbie-Anne for comfort. That is all I need to know. I go and assemble a posse, Sean Morgan and Will Howe and Matthew Park and his wife Vivian.

"I saw the open door," I lie, "and I knew something was wrong. One of the only times I've ever needed to draw my Colt in the line of duty."

Point-blank range, headshot, not even a time-active can get out of that one too easy.

"And while he was looking at you…" Rachel said.

"…you bashed him over the head with the chair," I finish. She'd had her eyes screwed shut then, too, and blood streaming down one arm. "Good teamwork."

"I was damn lucky I was in the neighborhood," Will says. "I was cruising by on my bike when I heard the shouting."

He'd also made sure that he was in the neighborhood at the time, took a special trip to do so. And after I made the citizen's arrest with my cuffs, he slapped on the *other* set of cuffs, the ones that only came off yesterday when he was released on parole.

While I was comforting Rachel and Debbie-Anne, and getting Rachel to the hospital for her cut, Morgan, Park, Will, Vivian and I were all tearing Lightfoot to shreds, body and worldline, in a deserted end of the state beach till I called halt. He was already discorded half out of time when we got him, but we have ways of making sure he felt every stroke before he was gasping for the air that refused to touch his sinner's lungs. Will and I drink a silent toast to Eternist justice.

"That's a hell of a story," Jessica says. "And you two married the next day, I take it?"

Rachel chuckles.

"Naw, it took another few months for us to figure ourselves out," she says. "But that's another story…"

So it goes. We finish up dinner, and finish the wine, and I serve coffee after. All the time, Debbie-Anne is looking at me with suspicious eyes that make me feel small. Even when I am turned away, I can feel her eyes on my back. Finally, our evening winds

down, I escort Amá to her apartment, and take my place at the door
to show everyone out.

Jessica is there first, in her little black dress from a time that
hasn't come yet. She offers her cheek, and I kiss both. It might be the
last time I kiss my Auntie Jessica goodbye.

"Goodnight, Gooch," she says. That's all. That's all she needs to
say, to say everything. She continues onto the porch, then stops and
considers, as if only now remembering something.

"By the way, I hear Hector Descanso's in town," she says,
turning her profile to me. "He'd like to see you. Soon. It's hard to
find the right time for old friends."

I nod, and she returns it, then continues her sashay out into the
night.

Will just offers a hand. The *gringos* here are a hugging people, so I
wonder why he is so formal. He nods at me, I nod at him. I think I
hear a second quiet flash as I close the door. It's when I lock it that I
realize how tired I am. I almost fall asleep then and there, with my
back to the door. Through the tiredness, I can feel the hairs on my
neck stand up.

I open my eyes, and Debbie-Anne is standing there, giving me a
funny look. Rachel's head is swiveling back and forth between us.

"I'm going to bed," Debbie-Anne says quietly. "You need
anything…you holler, okay?"

Something passes between the sisters that I do not understand,
and never will. Debbie-Anne flexes her wrist, and heads upstairs. By
tacit agreement, Rachel and I clean up in silence, blow out the
candles, turn off the fireplace. When we go upstairs, and she removes

her shirt for bed, I lay a hand on her shoulder, like a man does with a woman.

"Don't," she asks, almost a whisper. "It still hurts."

I nod, and I am glad she can't see the grimace on my face.

"Need an ice pack?" I ask her. "You want to be all right for your try tomorrow."

She starts to shake her head…then stops and nods.

I head back downstairs and get one of the cool-paks out of the freezer, wrap it in a kerchief, and bring it to her. I start to apply it, but she takes it out of my hands and puts it on herself. For a moment, I stand there with nothing for my hands to do. Then she and I lie down in our big, cold bed, and roll on our sides, facing opposite walls.

VII

April 19, 2014 – 12:01:29 AM

It takes a very long time for me to sleep. I am turning too much over in my head. Ratting out Hector, Debbie-Anne's glances, Rachel's scarf…María Ortega, Will's midnight trip, the coming nexus…and a dead Mexican on the beach the morning after tomorrow.

Why did Will lie about getting a knock at the door? What did he get at Rite-Aid?

What do I rat out Hector on? Have I done it yet?

María, how is she connected? Or is it, by some strange working of God, actually a coincidence that she showed up this morning?

What is Debbie-Anne thinking? Could she, somehow, be the one who strangles me? And why is she looking at me suddenly like I am Hank Lightfoot?

Lightfoot. I was hoping very much it was him. Without my lead suspect, there are a lot of questions floating around…and no answers.

I decide to follow up surveilling María in the morning, then double-up my afternoon for my own investigation and for Rachel's game. Nexus or no nexus, I am not missing Rachel's game. She'd never forgive me, and that's a hell of a way to die. Finally, I drift off to a dreamless sleep…the last full night's sleep I will ever enjoy.

I am up the next morning before Rachel is out of bed. She does not work at the health food store on Saturdays, and like all the McCoy clan she loves her sleep. The morning is clear and warm, the first glimmerings of the summer to come. Rachel looks like a little girl, her mouth loose on the pillow, her eyes softened and her jaw relaxed. She's thrown her arm crooked in front of her, the greens and purples blooming all along her soft, smooth skin.

I just lay awake and hold her for a long while. I don't know how long. Maybe not having clock-bugs can be a good thing, no? She nuzzles up into me, letting me rest my jaw in the curve of her shoulder and my belly rest in hers. She loves it when I rub her belly, my big overgrown tomcat.

She murmurs, and draws me in, holding on like she never wants to let me go.

After a long while, I worm my way out of her embrace, and start dressing. Every button I mark with a long look at my beautiful wife in our marriage bed. I am filled with a great sadness that I am missing breakfast, but I will let her sleep.

Debbie-Anne shocks me as I step down the stairs. She is awake, for one thing, and she is folded over the breakfast nook with a coffee, for another.

"Mornin', sugah." She turns around and sees who it is. Then, in a very different tone of voice, "mornin'."

"*Buenos dias, señorita.*" I say. "What are you doing up so early?"

"Y'know," she says, "stuff. You goin' out?"

"Business." I give her a rueful smile. "A detective never gets to choose his times."

She gives me that look again, the one that makes me feel so damn small. *Ay yai yai*, what have I done to deserve this?

"Just make sure you make it for Rachel's soccer game later." She says. "She's real angry with you."

Her eyes flick over my body, my powerful legs and swinging arms.

"Debbie-Anne," I ask, crossing to the breakfast counter, "what is going on?"

Rachel McCoy-Caballero never trembles, never cries. Debbie-Anne McCoy? Debbie-Anne McCoy *does* tremble. Her cup is rattling in her little hand, and something new comes into her eyes.

...is Debbie-Anne *afraid?*

"Nuthin', Gooch." She takes a pull of the mug. "Nuthin' at all."

I let the silence weigh on her, like a perp under question, but she doesn't seem willing to add anything. Another mystery to solve, *ay yai yai.* I go to the door, and put on my guns. They are loaded and clean. I throw the coat over one shoulder, and go out into one of the longest days of my life. Debbie-Anne's eyes follow me the whole way.

Outside, I hop in the truck and roll down the window. Then I think about where I am going, and roll it back up.

It's now 8:55 in the morning on Saturday. I would be too late to pick up María if I leave now. Fortunately, that is not where I'm going next. I set a rucksack, salvaged from the garage last night, on top of my briefcases on the passenger seat. For most times, a suit is best, because you can go down a few steps on the ladder by taking off your coat, removing your tie, and rolling up your sleeves. Not this time. This time, I need to go way down the ladder.

I play María's interview again as I drive, marshalling the facts, getting ready to play my part. Did she mention gunshots? No, and a soldier like her, she would recognize them. Only the flashes, that a man likes me recognizes as fourth-dimension spillover.

It is sunny and warm when I close my eyes, and foggy and clammy when I open them. Somewhere along the snaky byway that runs alongside Highway 1 as far as the Los Osos turnoff, my truck disappears, flashing in the sun. It is now just past 6:50 on Friday morning, and I am heading into town.

I park on the same little side street, and walk the two blocks up Nipomo to Higuera, huddling in my sportcoat and wielding the incongruous rucksack. It's even chillier, if it's possible, in San Luis this morning than it was back home in Morro Bay. I come in at 7:40, long after María's been sent away by the respectable people of West End Espresso.

In the back, calmly reading his Kindle and sipping some of the house espresso, is a suited Morgan. He must have appointments later today. He looks up at me with those fog-grey eyes, and nods.

I order a *caffe con leche* and a croissant, and sit down across from him.

"Good morning, Gooch." He says. "She came in at 7:16 and was waved out at 7:18."

I keep looking at him, and let the silence pile up. A good detective should be able to use silence and speech, whichever is most appropriate.

"Fine." He says. "I will speak to the owners about it."

I smile, and nod to him.

"Thank you." I say. "And do you have a package for me?"

He reaches into his Bill-and-Ted bag and pulls out a folder, sliding it across the table to me. It's thinner than I was expecting. It must read on my face, because Morgan speaks up.

"Her day appearance is as a Mexican immigrant laborer." He pauses. "She never quite gets the accent right, but passes well enough for some kind of Latin American. Such people are hard for me to track."

I know a few tricks myself, and I'm time-active. I could fake my birth certificate while drunk and blindfolded.

"Sightings?" I ask.

"Nothing definite, not that I could put together." He said. "She covers her tracks well, and when she doesn't, it is not in circumstances that lend themselves to handing over an amnesiac, how do you put it?, *joven*."

Chingao. I was hoping I could hand her to María's *vieja* easily enough. But there is an alternative, and I finger the card in my pocket. The look Morgan is giving me is very strange, and it is not helped by those eerie grey eyes.

"She goes by many names, but what is peculiar is that aside from the events involved in the next few days, she does not really appear among us." He means at the café, just up the street, where she is knocking on the door right now.

"So?" I ask. "Many of us don't. I come in on business. Elliot doesn't come in at all."

Morgan nods. His face is in want of a Cuban cigar.

"That is true," he says, "but in our business, it pays to be paranoid, doesn't it? That's why I checked up on your tomorrow..."

He stops there, as if afraid to reveal too much.

"If you are going to talk, talk," I say, "don't play pussyfoots with me."

His smile is soft and genuine. It looks good on him; I wish he would do it more.

"I'm afraid I can't." He says. "I've seen and heard, now I cannot talk. There is one thing, though, that I'm actually very happy to tell you: 10:39AM Saturday morning and eight seconds."

I feel my brow knit, take a sip of coffee.

"Why is that important?" I ask. "Something happen tomorrow, *señor*?"

"You think I don't pay a price for my line of work? I cannot be directly involved anymore." He says, looking into me with those fog-grey eyes. "Not until the posse is assembled. I know too much."

He rises to leave.

"But when you do assemble the posse…" He says, and he grins. It looks like a dog baring his teeth. "…talk to me."

"There is something I want you to do, after." I tell him. I meet his gaze.

"Yes?"

"When I am gone." I say. "Take care of Rachel. And Amá. You have my papers…"

"Of course, Gooch." He says. "If you aren't there, I'll see to their interests. You have my word."

"Make sure Rachel can have that trip to Britain she keeps talking about."

"Of course." His face shifts, I do not know how to explain it. He looks *human*. "And...goodbye, Gooch. It's been an honor."

It's as if something escaped him he does not want anyone to see. His mouth draws tight with shame. He turns, hiding his face from me behind his massive shoulders, and he walks out of West End Espresso. I finish my coffee, sipping contemplatively. I am going to be cold for a long time to come, it's nice to enjoy the close warmth and the taste of the *caffe con leche* while I can. When I am finished, I take my rucksack, and head into the bathroom.

Inside the briefcase is the outfit for a hobo, from the hiking boots to the worn-out jeans and Goodwill shirt and jacket. I change into the gear of the lost class, and even remove my shoulder holster. I stuff the gun in the back of my pants like a gangbanger, and leave my ankle holster where it is.

I brought my gun cleaning kit with me. I make sure both are clean and ready to go, and that I have spare rounds. They're in the fanny pack I'm taking on as part of my persona. I check the jeans, the fanny pack, is it too light? I check the shirt, practice my poor-man's English in the mirror. I look in the mirror. I ruffle my hair. I still look a little too clean. What's my story? It's 2014, down-on-my-luck carpenter who lost his livelihood in the Great Recession. That will go a ways towards explaining my middle-class behaviors and clean-cut appearance.

I am frightened. I am frightened to my toes. I have tangled with the Free Will before, but only in Active Service...not like this. And I was *dio a la Madre* then. It could be one, or it could be a tripod, or it could be a whole anarchist cell. I don't know. All I know is they're

Free Will, people who have no respect for the Twelve Laws of Time. They'll kill you as a child as soon as look at you. On the stakeout, María mentioned preemptively killing a man to take his house. A Free Will would. And it must be them. No one else would be targeting an innocent woman. And if she wasn't innocent, she would not be walking around free, whole, and unbloodied. She wouldn't even be a memory.

I look towards the creek, involuntarily picturing the scene. The trouble is if I surveil the battle first, I know what happens, and then I cannot change it. Like my death. It's why Morgan had to recuse himself from events. I'm running a little warm with Park, but then he'll always stand up for a fellow time-active, because Matthew Park wants to keep everyone safe.

I take a deep breath. I cannot be like this. I've only got so long before I fall down dead, and I'm wasting it in the bathroom. My cell phone says 8:23AM as I drop it in the rucksack. I close my eyes.

I open them in the early morning hours of Friday, in the parking lot behind the Oddfellows Hall. The lights are on, *no bueno*, but everyone's asleep or not looking. I take a long breath, and start walking. The Oddfellows Hall is on the street where I like to park, and it will give me a good look at the scene.

Nipomo Street, just before it crosses Higuera, goes over a bridge over San Luis Obispo creek. Also on the bridge are the old waterworks and Tonina's Mexican Food, which is passable and authentic enough when I'm drunk. On either side of the creek are the walkways, which the city spends absurd amounts maintaining, and the back side of all the bars on Higuera that the students love to visit on Thursday nights, and the restaurants and curio shops on Higuera their parents love to visit on Thursday afternoons.

The creek disappears under the buildings of Broad Street about fifty yards up…the Deep Dark, the underworld of San Luis Obispo. These places are a favorite of gangers, taggers and the homeless who pass through town, and it is here that María and I walked yesterday. My yesterday.

Now, the last of the bartenders are sweeping up after a Thursday on Higuera, and Friday is stalking in with its coat collar pulled up around its ears. It is damn cold for an April. After getting a good look from a few angles, I tromp down the Mission-side stairwell, descending to the creek itself.

If my timing is right, I have an hour or so before María appears. I make it down to the gravel, and realize that with the creek full of spring slush there's no dry passage to the next little island, under an old commercial block, where the homeless are going to set up their fire. I think I see someone moving in the darkness even now.

I curse, because I was hoping to keep my feet warm and dry. A detective lives on his feet, and I muse on this while I am sitting in the shadows of the creek walls removing my nice dry hiking boots and my nice dry socks. I have a working theory on where the *ingléses* went, and how they disappeared so fast.

I wade through the cold water, keeping one hand brushing the concrete wall on my left and making my ginger way past submerged rocks. *Chingao* it's cold. The water is only shin-deep, but I shiver up to the hairs on my head. And I must feel through the cold and shock or I will go down.

My feet are offering Pater Nosters when I step up onto another gravel island and the stately darkness of the concrete enfolds me. There are several buildings you go under, and beneath the first it is dark and quiet. I stop and listen, but there is only the spring-quickened sound of the creek slipping by next to me.

There is a shaft of the sickly orange-purple lightwash of the city at night ahead of me, and a spark in the darkness beyond. I can almost feel the kiss of the fire they are just now kindling. María must have miscounted the number of buildings she went under. This makes sense. One of my rules is that the client never tells the truth, although I like to imagine most of them try…well, except for that one woman who was setting me up to kill her husband.

There is another crossing I must make, under the shaft of light. I let the weight of the world settle on me like a poncho, then step slowly into the cold light. The fire is starting to crackle to life, there are five or six of them. I see slivers of cheek and feel wary eyes on me. I wince, throwing myself into my wincing, as my feet plunge into the water again. This time, they are nearly numb immediately, and I smack my cold-blunted toes into a rock or two. That will hurt like hell when they warm up.

I feel myself shiver. Shivering is good. I want my new friends to be *muy sympatico*.

I come up on the gravel, my feet slowly recovering from the shock and learning to feel pain again. I am still in the light, and they are looking to me, tense, waiting.

"Is there room by the fire for another poor bastard?" I ask, putting on an *ese* accent like a *chicano*.

One *gringo* with iron-grey hair and a clean shave smiles at me.

"Pull up a chair." He says. Everyone chuckles, and I come to sit down.

"I did not come alone." I tell them, reaching into the rucksack. "I brought my good friends, the Gallo brothers."

I pull out a bottle of fortified wine, "from Gavioty," for us to enjoy. It does not matter whether you are time-active or not: with a woman, a drink, or a hundred-dollar bill, I will open any door. The ironsides *gringo* politely declines, but the others and I all enjoy pulls from the bottle. I can only taste a little, I am on the job, but it does good work warming my bones. So does the fire, once it is up.

We huddle to the fire, and we drink our wine, and we shoot the shit. The older man is a profesh, a lifelong member of the homeless underworld. The girl on my left is a runaway who never finished high school back in Colorado. The beardless boy on my left was passed among aunts and uncles until they stopped checking up on him. There's two women about my age; one bitter woman who was once a real estate agent, one woman who I think is crazy. She mutters theories about 9/11 and the public library system.

We swap knowledge of when and where to find a bed for the night and get a hot meal. They mention a woman I know to be Alison, the "secret angel" who walks among them, and whisper of how she knows things, how she is there before she is needed. That is a useful bit of information. I put in a good word for Rachel's soup kitchen, and the place has earned five stars from the discerning elder statesman.

There is a flash in the darkness, under the next building. The runaway girl sees it too.

"*Ay yai yai*," I say, blinking and swiveling my head around, "what is in this wine?"

The girl seems about to speak, but changes her mind. Perhaps it is the wine after all.

I let the conversation flow around me, like the creek burbling a few feet behind, like the distant splashes of María coming to grips with herself, having just had twenty years of her life lopped off like the head of a chicken. The boy mentions the Anglican church over in Morro Bay, and he praises them, because when he and his two friends went there, the Anglicans treated them "just like anybody else," in his words.

The envy on the faces breaks my heart. Even the conspiracist, she wishes people would look at her without feeling disgust or pity or superiority. I must look into the fire then, and feel my heart sinking.

"What the hell is…?" The real estate agent never finishes her sentence. María has emerged into the light, looking half as disheveled as I remember, her shoes clutched in one hand. She looks around, her arms swiveling around her as she tries to figure out where she is. For a moment, she looks like a ragged angel, standing in the creek as if born to it and illuminated by the shaft of lightwash.

"Looks like another visitor." I say.

She spots the fire, us, me, and comes over, shoulders hunched, fiddling with her shoes. She turns them soles out to us, and then I realize: She is hiding her ankle knife. In case she needs it. She is otherwise the waif, the little lost girl, suspicious but not herself dangerous. Her eyes dart from the men to the women, not understanding.

"*Hola. ¿Eres el batallón británico?*" She asks, in a Catalan accent thick enough to roll in papers and smoke.

The *gringo*s all look around, then look to me.

"*El batallón británico?*" I ask. I switch to English. "What is that?"

"Britain…army." She says in the same language, shifting onto one foot. "Or German? You the Francoists?"

Headshakes all around. She visibly relaxes, balancing on both feet. I am glad, I have no doubt she could butcher all five of the *gringo*s with her little hand knife before they could alert the guards and it would be very awkward to stop her.

"Who're you looking for?" Asks the distinguished gentleman.

"I…do not know what happened." She says. "Which *barri* are we in? Which way is the *Palau de la Generalitat*? I must report in."

We all shake our heads. I feel the hardness forming, just under my skin. The mask I am wearing helps. I want nothing more than to invite her to sit down with us, to take her aside, to tell her in our own tongue that she is lost, the war is long over and Franco is dead, and take her away to Tonino's for a burrito and then to our guest bedroom. But I cannot. She has a date.

Sometimes, I hate the First Law of Time, too. It takes all my steel to let her wander away.

"What time is it?" I ask. The beardless boy checks his cell phone, and tells me it's 3:22.

She is behind me now, and I strain my ears. The conversation stumbles back to its feet, muted, with questions about María's sanity and a few quiet chuckles.

In my head, I count.

The first flashes come at 3:23:10. I can tell by the gasps.

"What the fuck is…?" Asks the real estate agent. The old gentleman jumps to his feet with the speed and gristle of thirty years on the road.

"*¡La policía!*" I shout. In the open, there are more flashes.

"Get that fire out!" The old man shouts, cupping creek water in his hand to throw over it. "Run!"

Everyone sweeps up bags and bundles and shoes. The old man takes the girl, who in her foolishness was running toward the battle. "Up the creek! Santa Rosa!"

Almost everyone splashes up the creek, except the conspiracist, who has fallen in the creek and is trying to stand. She screams, something is injured. While I reach toward her, my eyes are dazzled by María appearing in front of me, bloodied and filthy, blinking in surprise. She meets my eyes while the green spots are still dancing in them. I reach out and push her in the direction of the bridge, of the "restaurant with lights" and of the battle.

She is barely out of my hand when I see someone's back appear in another dazzling flash of light. I see his silhouetted arm raise up, María's knife glinting in his hands. *No you don't!*

I leap on him and there is another flash illuminating the scene: Our shadows struggling on the wall, the garish graffiti, the knife a deadly shadow, the little conspiracist looking up and crying and streaming her leg red into the cold creek waters. With arms that stopped horses in my youth, I yank his shoulders back, and we both land on our backs in the gravel and in the creek. He skips, taking me with him.

We appear two feet above the footbridge, and the cold amplifies the shock when I land, him in my arms. There are flashes all around us, him and me. I hear María yell, for a woman like her does not scream. I have him by the shoulders and wrap my legs around him, and we roll back and forth on the footbridge like a turtle. He knocks his head back into mine, and I see stars. We skip again.

Now we are two feet to the left. *Muy lamentablemente*, that is one story above the creek, and my back is down. I feel the air rush by, and skip.

We land in the creek, splashing, next to the skipping stones where there is a little waterfall. We separate and sit up, gasping for air. With a heave, I grab his head and smack it as hard as it will go into one of the stones. Now he's stunned and I can go to work. I reach in the back of my jeans and pull out my Colt.

He looks over my shoulder, and smiles. His *viejo*. I do not wait, I skip.

3:23:10, on the footbridge. I glance around, dizzy, cold, and I see him in front of me, on the Mission footpath, as María first sees him. There's a flash, and I do not wait, I skip. Now I am in front of María, as she pulls her knife. He is behind her and snatches it from her hands.

When the blade kisses her neck, I skip. The dazzle will make her blink when she instinctively skips away, for safety. For the "*batallón británico.*"

I am behind him, as he is behind María, and pistol-whip him. He spins around, sending the Colt flying from my hand, and I skip forward. Three seconds later, I watch: we are falling together. We skip in a flash of light, and I wheel around: María is running. I skip back two seconds, behind María, on the path.

"Run!" I whisper, and skip out again as she yells out.

I skip forward, five seconds, standing in knee-high creek water that is wicking up my jeans. In front of me, we appear, sit up, gasp. I crouch down. I move fast, without thinking, taking his head and slamming it into the stone. While he draws his Colt, I draw my .358 from my ankle. I stand, and the terrorist looks up into my eyes. My *joven* disappears in a flash, and I am left with my .358 at his head.

"Go ahead and try me." I tell him. "I will have a bullet between your eyes no matter who shows up behind me."

María heard no gunshots. There's no reason he needs to know this.

There's one last flash, on the stone where I slammed his head. Will is standing there, illuminated for an instant like an avenging angel. He has the cuff in his hand, a little cylinder about three inches long that dampens the capacity to time travel. He digs the end into the terrorist's shoulder.

"You could have Bill-and-Tedded it to me." I tell him.

"No, I couldn't." Will says, clapping a pair of regular steel cuffs on the man's wrists. Ah. The nexus.

"Fascist fucks!" The terrorist shouts. I wait, shivering without feeling the cold, my blood pounding in my ears.

"The cornfield?" I ask.

"The cornfield." Will's grin is tired, and frightened. And very, very false.

He disappears with his new charge, who is no longer capable of skipping on his own. Later, Will will tell me when the execution is, and we will all be there. This man just willingly broke the Sixth Law several times over, and I am sure Will's interrogation will reveal more.

I am wet and shivering and filled with blood and excitement. I feel *alive*.

I span back to break the Sixth Law myself.

I see the dying flash of my own entrance illuminating the tableau, our struggle together photographed on the far wall. We disappear together, and the woman is still bleeding out into the creek, weeping and freezing. I kneel down on numb legs, and pick her up with arms heavy as the adrenaline leaches from them.

"Close your eyes." I whisper. She does.

I have a spot behind the trees at French Hospital where no one goes. This is where I like to arrive when I need to visit French. There is false dawn in the sky, the shift is just changing over. My arms are aching, although she cannot be more than a hundred pounds…and she is soaking wet.

"They tried to get you." I tell her. "But We are fighting Them. You and I are at the hospital and you will be taken care of. But it is very very important that you do not tell them what happened. Do not tell anyone, not a soul. Say you fell down in the creek, say you were drunk, I do not care, but *do not tell anyone what you have seen.*"

She nods at me, and I carry her into the hospital.

What Morgan and Will and Park do not know won't hurt them. Or her. Or me.

I pass a handsome Mexican man with curly black hair and eyes the color of Jalisco earth loitering next to one of the parked ambulances. He nods to me, I nod to him. Her papers are filed and her stay is paid for by an anonymous donor.

When I have finally slipped away, it is already dawn, and all I want is some sleep or a bite to eat. But I have cleanup to do. I go back, and retrieve my Colt from where it clattered down the path. I haul up my rucksack while María is looking behind her, trying to see if she's being followed. I leave behind another toy Officer Park will not like me having: I slip the early 2030s flying bug from its little manila envelope and switch it on.

After changing in the bathroom again, I head down to the creek and pick it up, settling back on the gravel in the grey fog and playing back a three-dimensional image of María on fast-forward. I watch her enter the range, try to warm her feet, arrange the logs, all the way she said. I watch the flicks of light as she tries every match, and I watch her throw the book away in anger. 'It was frustrating,' hm? I can practically hear her howls of rage. I replace the bug in its little manila envelope, then skip after the matchbook.

As it drifts away the night before, I am there to meet it, snatching it out of the water. Hauling it up, I can read in the street light the name written on it: Happy Jack's, Morro Bay, California. Printed: 1958.

Eureka.

VIII

Rachel's scarf is off its peg when I come home for brunch. To hell with you, I saved a time-active and a mundane and I am going to die tonight, I deserve lunch with my wife. Even if it's breakfast for her. I hang up my coat, but I take my guns into my man's place. They are soaked through and need cleaning. I put them in the up-and-down drawer, and holster the clean set and hang them by the door.

She gives me a wag of the coffee mug as I cross through the house. I know what you're thinking, you're thinking I am still soaking wet and shivering from the creek. Well…sometimes having the café nearby is a blessing, too, even if it starts jokes going around about Will coming in soaked and muddy tomorrow.

Rachel made eggs Florentine this morning, with organic spinach and tangy hollandaise. Mine is on a plate, under the glass cover for the frying pan.

"Thanks fer callin'." She mumbles around her coffee. I make a note to call her later, when I pick up María.

"Where did you get the hollandaise?" I ask her, after making pleased sounds at the first bite. I do not have to try very hard. I have come home at just the right time, the English muffin is still crispy where my woman toasted it and the eggs and spinach are still piping hot. *Madre de Diós*, she is a genius in the kitchen.

"Uhhh…'round…" Her drawl is still thick, she has not put her voice on this morning. I know that voice, those pinking cheeks. She used a mix. I don't mind, but she thinks it is some kind of cardinal sin. Crazy redhead.

"You know why the meet's delayed today?" I ask.

"Somethin' about a baseball game? I dunno." She says. Then, with more authority: "I'm getting my try today."

"*Viva la mujare.*" I say. "You'll get it."

We eat in silence for a bit.

"Promise you'll be there?" She blurts out.

"Why wouldn't I be?" I ask.

"Oh," she says, sipping her coffee, "I dunno."

I find myself thinking of María Ortega, and I don't know why.

"Rachel-"

"Gabriel, I'm trying to eat." She says.

We do not speak again until I say "*adios*" at the door. By then, it is nearly eleven thirty.

Tidelands Park is down at the very end of the Embarcadero, not far from where I die. It's at the site of the old boat launch, and has rolling green grass and a playground with a great large pirate ship for the children. I used to dream of bringing my own children here.

I park the truck close by, and walk to the edge of the grass. In my shirt and tie, and with my briefcase, I look like a lawyer on his lunch break…or would, if it wasn't Saturday. Looking out of place, I keep walking, to the sidewalk over the bay, where it is sunny and beautiful. I watch the boats for a few minutes, letting the warmth into my bones.

Then I have the hackle-raiser, the feeling I am being watched.

"Gooch."

I jump back like it's an electric shock. The startle is like a force smacking into me. I whirl around and Debbie-Anne is standing there on the grass, nervously rubbing her bad wrist.

I curse freely in Spanish, then demand, "what are you doing there?"

She looks on, trying not to be amused. I do not know why she is amused. I was *surprised*, not *frightened*.

Something changes in her face. Something comes out of her, as if she reached deep to find what she needs. Something...

"Let's...sit down." She says, and gestures to a nearby bench. We go, and sit. It is hard and a little painful and very much the kind of park bench no one is meant to actually sit on. She sits on the other side from me, out of reach.

"What's up, *señorita?*"

"Gooch, I... I know what you've been doing." She says. She sounds as serious as I have never heard Debbie-Anne McCoy ever be.

I feel my heart in my throat, I am eating it. If she falls under the Sixth Law...oh *María llena eres de gracia, perdonarla por favor...*

"It's not that she told me." Debbie-Anne says, words spilling out of her. "Don't think that. She hasn't said a word, I swear. I figured it out last night. I know you're a decent man, so please..."

She looks me right in the eye.

"Stop hitting Rachel."

I cannot help it. I laugh big, full laughs. Debbie-Anne looks at me like I have sprung a second head.

"You think I'm..." The tears are starting to leak from my eyes. "...have you *seen* her? If I tried, I would be paste on the wall!"

"Gooch!" She hisses. "I saw her arms last night same as God an' everyone!"

I wave it off.

"She got those at rugby practice." I say, starting to get my laughs under control. *Madre de Diós*, I needed that.

"Oh yeah?" She demands. "When's that?"

"Tuesdays and Wednesdays." I tell her. "In the evenings. Santa Rosa Park over in San Luis."

"You're lying." She says, chomping down on my words like a dog with a bone. Or her sister with a scrum. "Wednesday was the potluck. She watchdogged me."

"Yes, because you came in on Wednesday morning." I tell her. "Not even Rachel's that dedicated."

"So why's she been wearing those long sleeve shirts?" She demands.

I take a moment to realize she's actually serious. She actually thinks I would strike my wife. Or that Rachel would let me.

"She works a register." I explain. "Short sleeves would make too many people ask questions like this. Besides, you know her, she might have some crazy idea they make her look weak. She wasn't afraid to roll up her sleeve last night, was she, telling the story."

"And that could be a cry for help."

"You know better." I tell her, trying to sound gentle. "Debbie-Anne, I am not beating Rachel."

She narrows her eyes at me, just the way her sister does. She does not know whether to trust me. And to think, for once I am telling the truth.

"Come to the meet this afternoon." I tell her. "If she hasn't already invited you. You'll see."

"No, actually, she's been pretty mum about her soccer game. She just keeps muttering about getting her try." Debbie-Anne says suspiciously. I do not have time for this.

A whole set of lies springs to my lips. I can see where the whole conversation will go, about discussing it on Monday, about confronting Rachel with it, and it all dies there with one thought: this is Rachel's sister. This is Debbie-Anne. I have seen her bruised and broken and I know why she wears a wrist-brace. She is trying to save her sister against a man she knows is armed and capable.

She may be little and blonde the way her sister is big and grand and well-built, but they are both strong in their hearts. I cannot tell her these lies.

"Deborah Anne McCoy," I say, "you know me. You know what I think of men like Hank Lightfoot, and what I do when I find them. I swear to you on my mother's grave that I have not laid a hand on your sister, who I love with all my heart. And I am glad that you have come to me about your concerns, because it shows me you love her too. You do not believe me completely, because you are also smart. After all, you confronted me in a public place just in case you were right. But come to the rugby game and watch your sister play. You will see where she gets her bruises from."

And what she does to them in return.

"It's not like I'm seeing her until then." I point out, after she chews on it for a moment.

"Gooch," she says, "I love Rachel. And I'm the only family she talks to more than once a year. I know both of y'all think I'm kind of a screw-up, naw s'true, lemme talk, but I won't stand for anyone hurting her the way he hurt me. I can't. And there's something *wrong* going on. You two have been at it since I got here. I've never seen her like this, all quiet 'n such. Makes me worried. Something's hurting her, and I don't think it's a stupid soccer game."

She's rubbing her wrist. Meeting my eyes. I am a little too shocked to reply at first. She has been... and that look in her eye... and *ay yai yai* all the lies...

Maybe I don't need my fists on her flesh. Maybe what I do is enough. The sun is bright and warm, a perfect day in central California.

"It is not going so easy." I confess. Even this much, even to her sister, I need to work a knife between my jaws to get them to open. "I don't know what it is. I don't know how to fix it. But I don't want her to hurt. I want her to laugh and run more."

Despite herself, Debbie-Anne reaches out and lays her hand on my arm. It's the hand with the broken wrist. Despite myself, her touch helps.

"I'll see you at the game." She confirms, standing up. "For what it's worth, I know you don't want to hurt her."

She walks away towards the playground, where the children shout. Park and his wife, Vivian, give me a few minutes to myself. Probably because I ask them to, sometime down the line. They are walking along the sidewalk, where it drops off to great boulders into the bay. Vivian's wine-dark hair is set well against a pale sundress, like she's a doctor's wife out for a Saturday walk. Park fits her, looking like a doctor out for a Saturday walk, all quiet, nicely-tailored button downs and jeans.

The Parks catch my eye, and have one of those chats with their faces. Park squeezes his wife's hand, and takes her purse when she proffers it. He strolls over to me as casually as if one of us is not dead on the beach tomorrow morning.

Park eyes me with a twinkle when he sits down. Something in his shoulders, in his eyes, in the way he walks...this is not my Park. This Park is much older, even if his face is ageless as a Korean saint statue.

"Just got the earful from your sister-in-law?" He asks casually by way of checking my whenabouts.

I just nod. Because if I said anything right now, he'd punch me. He chuckles.

"I'm not supposed to say anything," he says, "but don't worry about it."

"What do you mean?" I'm a detective, I am curious and ask questions. Officer Park smiles back at me. "Okay, fine. You get the scarf back?"

He reaches into his bag and pulls out the scarf, still wrapped in a plastic evidence baggie. The chain-of-proof card curiously omits the labs of 2036 handling it. I shove it into my suitcase guiltily, like this is a drug or arms deal.

"We smuggled the body up there, too," Park says, quiet enough, "as a Juan Doe. The nanites dissolved out on schedule, couldn't find a trace. Last meal was some kind of *pozole* and tortillas. Your knife scar from Hispanola's gone, too, and so's the scar from Paris; thyroid cartilage crushed by main force. Your sweat and your sweat alone was fresh on the weapon, Rachel's is in there, too, but too old to use as evidence. The murderer apparently wore gloves."

"That is very interesting, officer." I say. "Gloves means premeditation."

"It does." Officer Park agrees.

I do not say what else it means. It means I may live on borrowed time. If my scars are gone, I have had them removed. None of us have had to face discord, so we know that it is not my *joven* who is lying on that beach tomorrow morning. Besides, the knife-fight over Juana and the gold happened when I was a very young gun and new at the time-travel game.

Rachel may have a husband tomorrow after all, and that fills my heart with gladness. I may have a future. I may just know when and where it must end.

Or Park is not saying so much, so I think this, and can face my death with a little dignity. I feel my eyes squeeze shut, the muscles straining from the strength and from the length. No, Gabriel, that way lies madness. I have few enough friends, I need to trust the ones I have.

"Any other leads?" He asks hesitantly. He's treading on thin ice for the Laws of Time and on his own sanity by asking.

"Some." I say. "It could be Hector Descanso, from my time with Jessica. He is looking for me with a purpose and he is angry. Don't know how he could get the scarf, though. Will is acting strange, and why? I don't have a motive for him, though. It could be…"

The flash of hatred and hurt in honey-brown eyes.

"…María?" Park says, after the silence gets uncomfortable.

"She doesn't have a motive either." I note. "I am sticking my neck out for her. Why would she kill me?"

"Women, huh?" Park shrugs. His grin falls when he realizes what he just joked about. "Sorry, pal."

I watch the kids play, listen to their shouts, feel the warmth of the sun. It might be my last time.

"You're running out of suspects, Gooch." Park says, sitting forward. "Let me know if I can help any more."

"Do you know how it happens?" I blurt out.

He hesitates. What he says now, I must assume is true. And what he says, neither of us can change. But I must know.

"At this point in my life?" He asks. "Yeah."

"And you…" I swallow. "Rachel's been told."

"By this point? She knows."

"The other footprint." I ask. "The third man. Was there a third man on the beach when I die?"

His words are careful. "As far as I know…no. Only you and the murderer."

"Goddammit, *who is she?*" I shout.

Park blinks at me. "She?"

All the power runs out of me, draining out through my hiking boots.

"…he." I say, and even to me, my voice sounds tiny and crushed.

"You know I can't tell you." He says. "And you know why."

Because I would kill that *hijo de su chingada madre* where he stands right now. Or might. And then Will and Park and Vivian would have to circle around *me* in that deserted end of the state beach.

Several others would join them, come to town just for this, ones who did not feel conflicted about being there. I have made enemies as well as friends. Compared to having my worldline ripped apart while being beaten to death and crippled (assuming they left me alive after the discord), being strangled by an enemy does seem preferable.

"Gooch...you okay?" He asks, knowing the answer already. "Where are you going next?"

"Alison." I say. "I need to talk to her."

The relief is palpable. I watch Officer Park's hands drift away from his pocket, where he carries a time-active's cuff, and relax on his thighs.

"Good luck, Gooch." Park's smile is sad. "I'm on the posse already, when it's all over. But right now, I'm going to spend time with my wife."

There's a moment's hesitation. Then: "*Adios, muchacho.*"

He and I meet eyes, then shake hands. I hear myself say "*adios.*"

I wait a few minutes, and then spring up and do a set of push-ups in the grass. I feel the sweat, the ache, the blood pulsing through my arms and chest, the heat of the sun, the sharp grass. I can hear the lapping of the sea and the shouts of the children and I can smell the fresh sharp smell of the grass. I feel *alive.*

I breathe hard when I stand, glorying in the passing of my breath in and out of my lips. Back in the truck, I take a swig of water from the canteen I keep under the seat. I did not lie to Park, I am going to talk to Alison. I have a hunch there are no coincidences, not where time-actives are concerned. I put the car in gear, and make for San Luis Obispo.

Alison Wingate III presents as a history professor at Cal Poly, albeit one from a rich people. And it's true; the Wingates are very well-to-do back in Alison's hometime of 1908. The noble name of Wingate nearly died in the Great War, became destitute in the Great Depression, and effectively disappeared in the Bombing of Britain. Her papers on Victorian and Edwardian England are noted for their penetrating analysis, and like most of us up from our own time, she keeps quiet watch on her family line.

I would complain about the lazy *gringa* but for most jobs I just check my case notes stashed in 2022, have lunch at Dareda's Mexikorean, and then come back down here to walk the walk. Then again, most jobs don't end in my death.

First, though, I want to stop for lunch. It has been some time since the small little brunch with Rachel. Alison's house is close to the Grinder Shoppe, she lives in a duplex two blocks down. I pull into a quiet residential street (probably named after a tree) near Broad Street.

A glimpse of a tiny Asian man as I step out of the car is all the warning I have before I feel the warm little nuzzle of a weapon that won't exist for another fifteen years.

"Don't skip." He says from my passenger seat. "Scrambler. Get back in the car."

I climb back in the car. The scrambler looks like an early War model, more than capable of taking me out even if I do manage to skip away.

"Drive." He says.

"What's this about, Hector?" I say as I start the car. This is bad, but as long as he's talking, he's not shooting.

"You know damn well what this is about." He says, in the too-quick cadence of the '30s. "Head away from downtown. Which one did you tell?"

"Tell what?" I ask him. I delve deeper into the housing tracts between Broad and South Higuera.

"About me!" He's sweating, nervous, and likely to do something stupid. The little scrambler is shaking in his hand. I can only hope his stupid is not something that ends me early.

I might be able to skip in and get behind him, but the car is running along and it's a small cab. We're somewhere close to a nexus and I don't know if I can pull it off that precise. I decide to keep talking instead while I think.

"Hector, I know you are Asian-American, I know you are not born yet, I know you are a gambler who lost his gamble, and I know you twitch at the mouth when you bluff." I say. "The most interesting thing I know about you is that you and Jessica *chinga como los animals*."

His wide eyes are wavering. Has he been taking red-eye? Hector's gone down farther than I thought if he's messing around with red-eye. Red... there's a sign up ahead. Maybe...

"You're a fucking liar!" He finally declares, shoving the muzzle deeper into my ribs. "Someone's sniffing after Lara and there's only one way the fucking Time Cops could have found out! *Who did you tell?*"

We come to the sign, and I roll to a halt.

"Okay, Hector, okay." I say, and turn toward him. He's staring right into me, oblivious to anything else. "Is this how it is? I tell you, then you shoot me?"

There's no flash from the back of the truck. *Chingao.* I start accelerating again. If I cannot make it work at low speed, I might try high speed. It is not too far to South Higuera…

"You tell me," he says, "then I shoot you."

"This is not a very good deal, is it?" I ask philosophically. "I mean, for me. Either you shoot me, or I betray someone and *then* you shoot me. It will be very difficult for me anyway, as I cannot betray anyone, as I don't know what it is I am supposed to tell anyone."

"What'choo smoking?" He demands. "I got a goddamn gun to your ribs!"

"And I know I do not die today." I say. "I die tomorrow morning."

I sound more confident than I really am. He could very well shoot and put an end to me, and then everyone I love gets discorded all to Hell. I turn left onto South Higuera. Only a few more blocks…

"You're serious?" He asks, not believing. Apparently news of my death does not travel that far. *Lo encantador.*

"I'm serious." I say. "What's this all about, Hector? Who's Lara?"

"You know who Lara is." He says, shoving the warm scrambler harder into my ribs. I can almost feel his sweaty hand through my shirt. "You know her where and when. You're the one that picks her up."

"Hector, I am very far down my worldline, and unless I do that in the next few hours, you're talking to the wrong man." I tell him. I make a right turn, and thank Mary, mother of God that it's not Sunday.

On Sundays, the byway next to 101 where you can go to Sunset Drive-In is jammed with cars coming in and out, because Sundays are the swap meet. The cross street in front of the onramp would be buzzing with cars, and what I am about to do would not be possible.

"I got irrefutable fucking proof, man." Hector insists.

"What's that?" I ask him.

"You-"

I floor the truck onto the onramp. Lucky for me, the onramp is pretty flat, so I can get some good speed up. Hector isn't ready for the sudden swerve, and he swirls in his seat towards the door.

His shoulders go flying. His arms go flying. His gun goes flying.

I slam the brakes and skid to a halt next to the highway, narrowly missing going over the grassy bank. The engine chokes itself out, shuddering like a dying fish. My blood is up, my neck hurts a lot, my head is dizzy. Hector's head flies forward towards the dash. I grab a fistful of his greasy hair and help him. I help him a few more times. Lucky me he kept the gun in his right hand, and his body's in the way now.

I haul him back to see the blood coming off his pretty nose. He tries to point the scrambler at me but his eyes are all bleary. I grab the gun in both my hands and point it down towards the parking brake, feeling our sweat and every nerve tense to the possibility his slippery little hand will slide out between mine. His head comes forward towards mine, and I slam my thick skull into his nose again. His hand flinches, and there's a new scrambler hole in my car I will need to have fixed. The little gizmo falls from his hands, clatters under the seat.

With my right hand, practiced in the art, I pull out my Colt and use it as a tongue depressor. The scramblers, they are good killing weapons. But they do not intimidate like a cold barrel down your throat.

"Listen to me, *muchacho*." I growl. "I don't know any Lara. I don't know what you do. Whoever told you these lies is wrong. In twelve hours, I will be dead. I am not your problem, unless you continue to threaten me and continue to *make* me your problem. Certain people will know what happened here today. That is all they need to know."

I cock the gun.

"*¿Comprende?*"

Hector is the most predictable kind of dishonest man. He is always looking for his angles. It is why he was nervous confronting me…he would gain nothing.

Letting me go, now, that will gain something. His life.

He nods, very careful, very ginger. He does not want to make sudden moves.

"Open the door." He opens the door. Behind us, a car flies by.

"Get out of my truck." He moves very slowly, stepping out of the truck, not turning away. His eyes flick down to the seat. I lower my gun below the window, but keep it trained on him. "No."

Hector nods.

"Now, go down behind that tree. Take a piss. And then get at least ten years away from here." I tell him. He backs away, almost falling down the short slope of the bank. My phone starts ringing. I can feel my energy running out not to answer it, but I keep my gaze on Hector. He runs behind the oak, and doesn't come back.

I reach over, and close the door. Then I click the phone on.

"*Hola*." I say. I sound tired.

"Gooch, truck matching your description on the side of the 101 just past the South Higuera turnoff." Will says. "Weapons spotted. Get out of there."

I had the key turned before the word 'Higuera.' Something underneath the scrambler hole made a grinding noise.

"No." I mutter. "No no no no no…"

I look around, at the cars whizzing by. Too much traffic, too open. No way I'd be able to skip the truck out without being noticed.

I bow my head, and what happens next is between me and my God. I give the key one last turn and the engine starts up. The grinding sound disappears under the engine's purr, and I carefully pull out into, every tremble of the turning-over feeling like it will be the last. I take the next exit, onto Madonna, and in a few minutes the cops will arrive and find no truck, no guns, and no men. Soon, I have nursed the truck back to a quiet residential street, probably named after a tree, just off of Broad.

The Gaslight is open. I walk in, wash off, and order a tequila. Normally, I don't drink on the job, but fuck my day. I'm drinking.

After the shot has hit me, I think I am thinking more clearly for having had whiplash. It hurts like hell, yes, but I also have a white logic to the case.

Not Lightfoot. Not Hector. Almost definitely not María. The list of time-active suspects is getting very short, but too much doesn't add up for it to be someone who isn't. Or maybe I just want to think that. There's only one way to solve a case, though, and that is with information. Joey the barman collects my money, and I walk out to stop by the Grinder for a late lunch and then go to Alison's.

The sandwich sobers me up a little, something I'm glad of right now. And it gives me a chance to mentally organize and prepare for my interview with Alison. This is not a social call, whatever I need to tell her. And it won't be fun. Suddenly, I wish I was less sober.

I walk the two blocks down from the Grinder to Alison's. She lives in a duplex on South Higuera next to a very strange couple of married *gringos*. Modest, but well-kept. Little yard. Alison's Mini Cooper. Closed shades. It is a nice little place. I knock.

"Gooch!" she says, after opening the door. "This *is* a surprise."

She sounds a little worried by that. Alison is the kind of time-active who is not used to surprises, and the kind of woman for whom surprises have usually been bad.

"Good afternoon, Alison." I say. "May I come in?"

"Of course." she says, the prim British tones of her upbringing telling. "Tea?"

"Thank you." Her living room is simple, yet affluent. There are flowers in a vase before an easel...I never knew Alison painted...shelves of books on history, culture, literature that I have never gotten around to, a TV gathering dust, a desk with a new Mac on it, and a nice, supple couch surrounding a dark mahogany coffee table. She gestures for me to sit.

"Got the kettle on," her accent slides back into the American one she has adopted, "now what brings you to see an old lady like me?"

"You are not so old, *señora*." I tell her. My upbringing tells, too. I reach in my pocket and pull out a notebook. "I wanted to ask a question or two, actually."

I reach around my pockets, but my pen seems to have gone. Must have lost it fighting with Hector.

"Let me find you a..." she reaches in her purse, "oh *drat*."

I watch her eyes come unfocused for just a moment, then she reaches in her pocket. She pulls out a beautiful pen that would cost more than a whole divorce case for me.

"Now,"

"Alison..." I ask, sounding casual. "...what time on Thursday night did Will call you in? For the cleanup of the twinning?"

She has to think on that for a moment, looking for the answer on the ceiling.

"About four thirty." She says. "Why?"

"Just a moment." I tell her. "Can you tell me where it was?"

"Yes, I can." She says, in the voice Sister Juana used to use with me when she caught me chewing tobacco at school. She does not elaborate.

"If you want," I say, "I can have Officer Park draw up an official request. Or Will."

I watch her jaw opening just a bit and then slowly closing again, but not all the way. She is biting her tongue, the way she does when she is nervous.

"I think they would be very interested in a rumor I heard among the unfortunates." I smile congenially at her. Rachel calls it my perp smile, and notes it is very offputting because my eyes are not smiling. At all. "A rumor about a secret angel, and quiet whispers of her powers."

"You wouldn't *dare*." She says, her eyes hardening.

"You know the Laws of Time as well as I do." I say, and now my eyes are smiling too. "Alison...I understand. You know how I feel about people who are not blessed with our gifts."

I let that sit, and she looks on me with approving eyes. I have married one of the little people, aren't I *un buen caballero?*

"I think what you are doing is good work." I add. "Because it shows you have true nobility of soul, and still have the common touch."

In her days, during her youth, those were the words of praise for women like her. She places one hand lightly over her breast.

"We do owe something to them." She says. "Our gifts give us the power to help them more, and I think we have to. But between the officers and that convict's son...they don't *understand*. You're possibly the first man who does."

"So, sandwiches left in their cars while they're out?"

"And resumes sent in anonymously." She preens. "Warnings about raids. I don't know how those folk would manage without someone like me to look out for them."

"So..." I say. "Now we know where we stand. I don't want to talk to Will or Park about this, but I would like to know some things about that situation on Thursday night."

Will had her convince a couple of observers that they didn't see a *veijo* and a *joven* together, what we call a twinning. She fixes her eyes on me. Yes, it is blackmail. But I am also being polite about it. And besides, I understand her feelings for the mundanes, for the little people, don't I?

"Morro Bay." She says. "South Morro Bay. I'm not sure where."

Now for the clincher.

"Alison..." I ask. "Whose twinning was it?"

"You promise nothing said leaves this room." It is not a question. It is a command. I just smile.

She sighs ostentatiously, and runs her hand through her fine grey hairs.

"Will's." She says, leveling her eyes at me, a grin spreading across her hollow cheeks. "He swore me to silence, but we all bend the Laws every now and again...don't we, Gooch?"

Yes. Yes, we do.

IX

April 19, 2014 – 8:57:22 AM

First, I drop off the truck at my mechanic. He jokes about having never seen damage like that before, but by tomorrow he will have ordered the new parts and installed them and forgotten all about it. Now I have a nice nondescript rental, and am on my way to pick up María.

I sit in the parking lot and make a couple of phone calls. First I call Morgan and Park in Morro Bay, and ask Morgan to make some 2Dogs Coffee and Park to pick up a bagel with cream cheese. I remind Morgan that he owes Jerry a call sometime in the next few days.

Then, I call Jerry myself, and make sure things are in place.

María is coming out as I finish placing the Bill-and-Ted order, her shopping bags a little more full than they were last night. She is again wearing jeans, this time with a black tank-top. The red shirt is over one arm.

"*Buenos dias, María,*" I say, opening the door for her. She is confused.

"What happened to your truck?" she asks, eying the new roundness of the rental's interior. It is nice to hear her lifting old world Spanish accent.

"Had a bad encounter with a bastard from the 2030s." I say, waving it off. "Just as good, though. Come on in."

She throws her bags in the backseat, where I can see a towel peeking out of one of them. She catches the drift of my gaze, and smiles.

"Liberated for the People." she says.

"How much is left in the room?" I ask. The car hums to life where the truck would tremble.

"The bed," she replies lightly, "and the toilet. Where are we going?"

I reach back, and grab my briefcase. Inside, along with my usual equipment, are two used evidence baggies.

And another evidence baggie with a woman's scarf in it, stabbing me with its implications.

I pull out the smaller one, and show it to her.

"Look familiar?" I ask. She takes it in hand, pinching the corners lightly, scrutinizing.

"The matchbook," she looks back up at me.

"Slightly waterlogged, but yes," I say, "combined with the card, I am pretty sure I know where to find you, and how to send you home."

Her smile is genuinely happy. And genuinely sad, somehow.

"And how is your case going?" she asks.

"I'll tell you when we get to 2002." I say. "I am out of practice and can just about make it that far. But that will be it for me. It's been a busy morning and I don't think I can go much farther."

She looks around.

"What year was this car made?" she asks. Ah, she is a clever one.

"2001." I tell her. "Once we go farther downtime, we'll have to leave it. Do you mind alternating?"

"So you take me downtime, then I take you downtime?" she asks. "I don't mind, but I don't know how far I can go."

"We'll find out." I say, putting the car in drive. It will be a good test for her, find out how well she swims in these waters. "We'll go down as far as we can, then get a few hotel rooms."

"Already?" she asks.

"Trust me, you'll be tired." I tell her, as we pull onto the street. "But we can walk around some, if you like."

"I think I would." What was that in her voice? I cover by making the last and most important phone call.

"'ullo?" It's 9:18. Rachel must be brewing her first mocha.

"*Buenos dias, amor mio,*" I say, before switching to English. "I'm wrapping up a case that couldn't wait, but I should be home for brunch around ten thirty. Whatever you have cooking, will you make some for me?"

"'kay..." she says, only half-registering.

I want to tell her I love her. I want to tell her I miss her. I want to tell her a lot of things. But I can feel María watching me, and still hear that something in her voice.

"See you for brunch." I say.

"See ya." she echoes.

I click it off. María is still watching me.

"Weekend trip to the 1950s and back in time for breakfast, hm?" She says, lifting one of her dark brows.

"Oh no," I say, "I already went."

My phone rings again.

"*¿Hola?*" I say.

"Exterminated in María's room." Officer Park says. Code: He's picked up the flying bug from 2036. "Gooch-"

"We talked about it at the rendezvous," I say, in my nice professional voice, "we can take it up then?"

I can see, in my mind's eye, Park rubbing his nose the way *gringos* do when they want to keep a secret.

"Okay."

"See you then." I tell him.

"You are popular today," María says, "I'm jealous."

"Ask my wife," I say, a little more pointedly than I need to, "she is jealous, too."

We make it the rest of the way to Morro Bay in silence. We pull into the parking lot on the little strand of beach next to the Natural History Museum. It's less a parking lot than just some cleared sand, but it works for our purposes. It's the perfect time: too late in the day for clamming, too early for casual visitors.

María looks on, hand-rolled cigarette dangling from her lips.

"This is where you die." she says. I nod to her.

"This is where I die." I pull out the manila envelope from my briefcase. "And *this* is what will see."

She smiles.

"Very clever." she says. "So we will skip up to tomorrow and see what's on the tape, yes?"

"No." I say, as we get out of the car. "What we see on the tape is what happened. There would be no way to avoid it."

"It's your life, Gabriel!" she says. "You are going to protect your delicate sensibilities about free will at the cost of your life?"

"I am going to protect my life." I say. "The less precise details I know, the more I can decide them."

And the more I can perhaps escape them, at the cost of buying time. I hand the flyer to María.

"Go put this over on that eucalyptus," I point to the one where I stand tomorrow morning, considering my own dead body.

Somehow, I find myself at what will be the scene of the crime. Without a word, smoking like a soldier, María walks up to join me.

"This is where it happens?" she asks.

"This is where it happens."

She looks around.

"Show me."

We spend a few minutes walking around, while I outline the scene of the crime for her. Another car pulls up, a family, black man and white wife and their two children. I think they think we are doing some kind of theater.

I realize that I will never see children in my house. I could not have any of my own, but I had dreams of maybe adopting…something Rachel and I would talk about. As they walk down to the beach, María tosses her cigarette in the sand and we go back to the rental.

We drive in silence up the slope, past the golf course, parking in the lot halfway up Black Hill. There's one other car parked in the dirt, but no one around.

"Okay," I say, "grab everything. We'll see how far downtime we can go."

She takes her two bags, and I grab my briefcase and the backpack, now filled with clean clothes and other equipment for a few days in the past. I make sure to take out my Bluetooth and drop it in, unless I want very funny looks in the 1990s and a stern warning from Officer Park.

"You are lucky you are not very fashionable," I say, before clicking the lock, "your outfit will pass for decades."

"Fashion is *bourgeois*," she replies simply. "So, where is our private nook for skipping through time?"

"My favorite spot is right up…here." I say. There's a little copse of trees along the hiking trail that really is my favorite spot, since it's hidden on three sides and the fourth looks out over the Estuary and Los Osos. Nothing but wide rolling California hills as far as the eye can see. And not even the teenagers think to neck here.

I shift my briefcase to my other hand, and María takes my hand in hers. First, our eyes meet, and then she screws hers shut. I peg a nice spot in 2002, and blink.

It's early afternoon when I open them again. The hills were green when I left, now they are brown and dusty as Baleños in the summer. I feel tired, dog tired. I lean over a bit on the little Spaniard with the muscles like steel cables.

"Are you all right?" she asks.

"Tired," I say. "I've been skipping around a lot and I think I'm out of juice. Give me a few minutes. How far do you think you can go? Think you can hit 1991?"

Her other hand brushes against her stomach, like a pregnant woman thinking of her child.

"No...I feel like that is too far," she says. "Let me try five years, and see if I am just as tired as you, *mexicano perezoso*."

I find just enough energy to chuckle. Our eyes meet, and I let the heavy lead fall over mine.

When I open them again, the hills are the quiet grey of the early spring, before the rains have come. We are standing together, leaning into one another. I can feel her muscles against mine, and, tired as my body is, it is still a man's body. I let go of her, step back.

"How do you feel?" I ask.

"Like I just sprinted across *la Plaça de Catalunya*," she says. Her tiny frame is heaving with breaths.

"Hand me the bags." I ask.

"I didn't take your briefcase when you skipped."

"You want to, go ahead next time."

She hands me her shopping bags, and stands stoop-shouldered for a bit, panting.

"Come on," I say, "there is a good place to get coffee just down the street."

She slides her arm around me, and I put my arm over her shoulders. She holds me not as a woman but as a comrade-in-arms...I appreciate it. Arm-in-arm, we walk down the path, onto the street, past the golf course club house, and walk into town.

We stumble past the windmill house, past the fish market that's long-abandoned in my time, past the artists' cabins scratching the hills among the eucalyptus trees, past the eucalyptus stand that will be *Californio* tract housing in a blink, into the quiet, aggressively proud little town center. It is 1997 and all is right with the world: 2Dogs Coffee is open for business.

We separate, and come into 2Dogs as it was, with its three funny old computers and strange painting and its burled bar, loaded with consigned baked goods, with a "quirky" barista. I stand behind a very loud *gringo* in a leather vest who looks like he could be Uncle Jerry' brother, slowly convincing the barista that he wants four shots of espresso in his coffee.

He manages to convince her, and she even takes down the board on the wall and writes, below the two-shot "Bad Dog," the "Rabid Dog" with its four shots. It is that kind of place.

"Hi there!" she chirps as the man departs with his coffee. "Welcome to 2Dogs! Can I help you?"

I order my *caffe con leche* and María, her Spanish black coffee. She is fortunate the barista can speak Spanish, I do not think she could express her preferences otherwise. The barista even compliments her on her softly-lisping accent. I pick up two of those English scones, as well, and pay in cash.

"What's this?" María asks, after we have sat down. She takes a nibble.

"In English they call them 'scones,'" I tell her, "they seem to be popular with coffee now."

I take a secretive glance around to make sure no one is eavesdropping.

"In a few years, it will be Starbucks time and it will be Italian this, Italian that all over," I whisper, "but for now they are happy to be *los ingléses*."

She smirks a devil's grin and takes another bite.

"Are we marching all the way back to that hill before we go farther?"

"We don't have to. But I like how private that area is. Never can be too careful about the Sixth Law." I say. "Are you up for more today?"

"I *think* so..." she says. "But I don't know how much farther. Definitely not 1991."

She can make something just less than ten years. That means she's about as well-trained as I am, and I am a bit narrow for a rank six. Maybe she is rank four or five, or a rank three who keeps in practice doing these kind of long skips.

"We'll wait half an hour, drink our coffee," I say, "then take a bathroom break, *¿si?*"

"*Si*," she replies, sipping her coffee.

We talk for a few minutes of nothing very important, and I quietly admire how silly everyone looks in their 1990s fashions. As we finish up, I feel more awake myself... enough to skip maybe a year, maybe a little more, but I would rather take it easy.

"Ready to go?" She asks.

"*Si*," I say, "the bathroom is in the back, on the left behind the pillar. You go in. In a few minutes, I will follow."

She walks off with her bags and almost goes into the office before finding the bathroom. The long-haired *gringo* in the office seems a little confused. I try Will's number, but neither his phone nor mine is active yet. I stand, and nonchalantly head for the bathroom. I slip behind the pillar and give a knock.

"¿*Si?*" María asks. "Sorry, I am reading mysteries on my stakeout."

"Because they are not very interesting, no?" I ask. She opens the door just enough for me to squeeze in with my things.

"Ready when you are." I tell her. She shifts one bag to the other hand, and holds out her free hand. I hand her my briefcase, then take hold of her free hand. I close my eyes.

When I open them, it's pitch-black. I can feel the darkness around me, then I can feel her leaning on me, the length of her body against mine. It is unsettling.

"…when are we?" I ask.

"Uh, 1993?" she says.

"Aha," I say, "then this building is not yet occupied."

I feel around and the bathroom walls are not there.

"Come on." I say. "We need to skip across."

"…across?" she asks.

"Same time, different place." I say. "Grab everything."

I can feel her warmth along my body, her hand in mine. I blink, and we're back in the copse. The sun is just above the water beyond the sand spit, and the first whisps of chill are coming in.

"I think it's time to get a hotel, ¿*si?*" I say. María nods, and as the weariness falls from her, she straightens up. Just another march for this soldier. We march down through town, stopping only for me to buy a bottle of Johnnie Walker Black, and come to a motel run by a nice Chinese couple.

The trouble comes when I reach for my wallet. On my credit card, embossed, are the numbers "06/11." As in 2011. It is now 1992. I smile, and ask how much for a single.

"Problem, Gabriel?" María asks.

The price is just about what I have in cash. I keep talking to the woman while I set the money on the table, and pray I have one of the old twenties on top. The nice Chinese woman does not notice the year of the twenties, because the old one is on top and because she is busy looking at the shining gold wedding band on my finger. And the lack of any such band on María's.

"Thank you," I tell her, taking the key.

"She thinks I am your mistress," María states while we cross the parking lot to the room. She is loud about it, but even so, she is saying it in Spanish.

"Yes, she does," I say, embarrassed.

"How old is your wife this year?"

"1992?" I think for a moment. "Four."

María tilts her head.

"And I'm an old woman," she grins.

"And you're helping me on my case," I tell her, putting the key in the door. "I usually do this alone, but…"

I leave it unfinished as we move into the little motel room. There is the nice bed, and some chairs and an end-table. And a little desk. I take out the flash cards, the thumbtacks, the string, while María is unpacking the toiletries she liberated from twenty-two years in the future. As I am setting up, she comes and sits on the bed, looking on with unabashed curiosity.

"Here's what we have," I say, "my body on the beach, over here."

I tap the flashcard tacked to the wall.

"Easter Sunday, 7 a.m., 2014." I continue. "Evidence says I died between 1 and 3 a.m. There's two men on the beach at that time, maybe three."

"Big difference."

"*Si*, but it was only part of one footprint, it could have been a beachcomber from earlier." I say. "We also found some cigarettes, mostly Camels. The murder weapon was a scarf."

I reach into my briefcase and pull it out, toss it to her.

"This scarf."

"Your wife's," she says. It is not a question.

"Death by strangulation with a broad cloth. That was in Morgan's hands. He says his *viejo* drops it off with him."

"Why haven't you mentioned him as a suspect?" she wonders aloud.

"He is a methodical man." I say. "He would not strangle a man in a fit of passion."

I have seen him kill. He would do it with his bare hands. Or from behind with a steel pipe.

"The body was moved. At least turned over."

"And given the suspects we have, you could be killed anywhere or when," she says.

"But there's signs of a struggle at the site. So either the body was fought over..." Or I died there. But then why turn the body over?

"How do the detective fictions put it? Means, motive, and opportunity." she muses.

"Everyone had the opportunity. Time-actives."

"Everyone, you mean, but your wife." Her eyes meet mine, and it feels like her knives seared into my eyeballs. "Gabriel, you have to look at the facts. She has the means and the motive. If she has the opportunity, you have to accept the truth."

"It was not her."

Now the anger is in her eyes.

"You are a romantic," and she spits the word out like a curse, "Francisco was a romantic and it got him killed. Gabriel, you tell me you want me to help Park find your murderer and bring him to justice. I will give him, or her, a tribunal's justice, but I will not kill an innocent man to spare your feelings. There are enough people in the world willing to do that, but María Ortega does not."

We stare across the narrow floor for a long time. Then I stand.

"Roll your cigarillo," I tell her. She yanks the tobacco from her pocket and starts rolling, fixing her eyes on it. I take out the bottle of Johnnie Walker and pour myself a drink with one of the hotel coffee mugs. Two fingers. I talk while I work. "Hector has already attacked me. He knows that he was wrong, and he knows better than to try again until he is certain that I have done what he wants to attack me for. Lightfoot has run, very far and very fast. So they are out. For a moment, I thought it might have been my sister-in-law. She does not blow her top like Rachel does, she lets her anger build up."

María and I meet gazes. I cross over in two steps and sit at the desk again. Our eyes never leave.

"Such people are very dangerous," I say. She smirks, and pops the cigarillo in her mouth. She leans over, rolling her lips back and chewing the end between her teeth. Like a good *hombre*, I flick open my Zippo and light her up. She smokes normally, the cherry glowing before her face.

"So who does that leave?"

"You, Will…" I take a gulp. There is no saliva, my throat rasps. "…and Rachel."

I wash my throat with the whiskey.

"I am not going to kill you, Gabriel," she says, blowing the smoke out her nose.

"I would not be sitting here talking about it with you if I thought you were." I say. Then, I lay out the facts, as casually as I would open up my gun for cleaning. "Why do you think I talked about killing a time-active with you? You don't strangle with a scarf. You would kill with the knife you wear at your ankle, slipped into the heart or shoved through the throat. From the back, if you could help it. I died on my feet. I died fighting. You would not let me die fighting."

She meets my gaze, but it wavers. Her hand is very very still. Too still. She is suppressing the fear, but she feels it.

"And Will?" she asks.

"He's been acting strange…mysterious twinnings, movements in the middle of the night. But he has no motive." I say. "We have been partners for years. He has had a thousand opportunities to kill me or leave me to die. We have fought shoulder to shoulder, gone blow for blow against the Free Will together. I might as well suspect Matthew Park."

"*Los compañeros*." she says. Comrades. The word is full of life and love. I nod to her.

"What about that woman you mentioned?" she asks. "Jessica?"

"We would not be here discussing it." I say. "There would be no body. The Legion would have cleaned up after her."

"Like the *Falangistas*." She actually does spit, and the carpet darkens where it landed.

I look at my board, at the lines, at the cards. When she clears her throat, I turn back to María, setting the scarf aside.

"And..." I slap myself. "*Ay carumba*! The scarf! They haven't brought it back! So it can't be *any* time-actives, they would have returned the scarf when they were done with it...and Debbie-Anne's already out..."

That leaves one last possibility.

"It can't be..." I say, "...but it must be. *Que será, será*. It must have been Rachel."

Rachel... *Madre de Diós*, Rachel...

My own wife...! My own wife is the one to murder me in hot blood. I cannot believe it. I do not want to. My heart leaps up in my throat.

"Is it bad? I am more worried about her than about me." I say. "I know I die. I know how. But what they, what you, will do to her...what kind of man does that make me, to let that happen to her?"

"It makes you a man in love," María reaches over, lays her hand over mine. Over my wedding ring. "I'm sorry, Gabriel. I do not know what I would do if I knew ...if I thought Francisco killed me."

I finish the whiskey all in one slug.

"I don't know." I say. "It's only a theory. She does not necessarily have the opportunity. We know she is in bed at seven o'clock the next morning. Murderers do not usually go home and sleep the night through."

"She might have been tired," María suggests. I shake my head.

"No, she is too smart for that." I tell her. "She would at least go to a hotel. My woman, she has a lot of smarts. She went to college and studied history and math."

"Why haven't you given her the *cabaceo* yet? She sounds perfect for this kind of life." María asks. She takes another thoughtful puff between her teeth. "Perhaps in her future, she *does* time travel, and came down here?"

"I would be most likely to *cabaceo* her," I explain, a hitch in my throat, "so that's out, but the rules are ...complicated."

And it would expose her to more men like Lightfoot. I study the board again.

"How do you do that thing where what you need is in your pocket? I'd like to slip a flask in one of mine." María asks, rolling a new cigarette. How long have I been lost in the collage of yarn and tacks and cards?

"Ah, you mean a Bill-and-Ted," I say. "Simple. You promise yourself, or write down, or something, that you will go back and put it in your pocket before you check."

"Isn't that changing history?" she asks. "Your ...Rule One."

"It isn't, but it can discord you if you're not careful," I tell her, "and you shouldn't do it more than one at a time, it's impolite to your *vieja*."

She nods, and offers me her unlit cigarette end. I light it for her again, and watch the smoke curl around her face, before her dark cunning eyes...

I could really use another drink.

"Would you like a drink, María?" I ask.

"*Si, gracias.* Why kill you on the beach?" she asks. "She could just as easily kill you at home."

I lurch to my feet and busy my hands with pouring myself a second Scotch, as well as one for María.

"Throw off suspicion?" I suggest.

"Not very well if she used her own scarf." she takes another puff, gears turning behind her eyes. "And I thought you said it was a crime of passion?"

"Matthew Park mentioned today the murderer must have worn gloves. That's shows planning, not passion."

"Does your wife wear gloves?"

"No."

I pass her one of the mugs as I sit down again.

"*Muchas gracias*, Gabriel. If it is her..." she says. "I'm sorry you see your faith in her and your love for her rewarded like this."

"Thank you, comrade," I mutter. María raises a glass.

"*A tu salud.*" She grins. To your health. Even as I am, I chuckle and raise my coffee cup full of Scotch.

"To yours." We drink.

"It's not a crime of passion," María says, our little break over.

"And she would be smarter about it if she were preparing at all," I say. "Just wearing gloves and bringing me out to the beach…people can be stupid, but she would have at least brought a weapon."

"Looking for holes, Gabriel?" she asks, sucking on her cigarillo.

"Looking for the truth." I tell her. "Too many things about Rachel doing it don't add up."

"You said yourself nobody's returned the scarf," she says, "and any good time-active would have. Or any good murderer who is time-active."

We sit and sip our Scotches a few minutes. She smokes down her cigarillo. I turn over the suspects in my head, moving cards around, moving tacks, looking for new connections. Moving them around physically helps, even if sometimes not even I can decipher the mess I've made of them.

"Do you really think there's a secret connection between Hector Descanso and your sister-in-law?" María asks at one point, skepticism all over her voice.

"*Madre de Diós*, I hope not." I say. "Even Debbie-Anne has better taste in men than that."

She chuckles, and I turn around to get a look at one of those fleeting smiles she's heard other people speak of. She is just tamping down another cigarillo.

"Three cigarillos?" I ask. She shrugs.

"It's a three-cigarillo problem," she replies, sticking it between her lips. I offer my lighter again, but she pushes it gently away.

She stares at the wall, as if expecting snipers to emerge from it. Slowly, she slides her hand down her coat, brushing against her body, and into her pocket. A grin spreads across her face, and her eyes flick down to the cheap little green lighter she's wrapped her hand around.

That's when I know.

"It *could* be one of us..." I say. "It could be one of us who *can't* return the scarf, because they're running out of time. Someone who can't afford to go slipping around at random dotting i's and crossing t's. Someone who can't Bill-and-Ted. ...and who wouldn't call Uncle Jerry because of the necessary question of disposing of a murder weapon."

She inhales her tobacco.

"Like who?"

I shake my head.

"It can only be one man." I say. "Will."

X

June 4, 1992 – 7:20:33 AM

While María sleeps, I hunt in the darkness for a way to test my suspicions. If only I had left some kind of test back in 2014! Then it hits me. I *did*.

There is a knock on the door in the morning, during our morning coffee. When I open it, it's Uncle Jerry and a little grey man in a sober suit.

"Come in." I tell him. María sips coffee in the corner, to no particular comment from Uncle Jerry. The money-man, he looks over María with disgust, who returns the look with interest. "What brings you?"

"You do." Uncle Jerry says, and I realize here is a much younger Jerry. His hair is a cloud of darkness, not a cloud of grey, and the lines of his face are not drawn so deep. "Brought your money man."

I sign the promissory note for $500 per decade, 1951-1991, all issued in the first year, as I should have done first. He completes his business, tips his hat, and quietly skips away.

"And news from 2014," Jerry continues, "Matthew Park's none too happy about it, but he checks the bug you left on the beach..."

"When?" I demand. "It is very important."

"About six in the morning. A nice US military flying spy bug from 2036."

María watches us like she is watching a ping-pong game.

"It's not there?" I ask. I cannot contain my excitement.

"It's not."

Inside, I am confused with feelings, hot and cold and up and down…I feel like if I tried to skip, I would burst into atoms. Rachel is innocent. She's *innocent*!

"*Gracias*, Jerry." I tell him. There are tears I am not crying. They are in my throat. "*Muchas muchas gracias.*"

"*De nada*," he says, "keep on trucking, my friend. We can talk later."

He quietly lets himself out while I let my feelings wash past.

"What was that?" Maria asks, setting her cup down. We settle back into Spanish, talking as we prepare for our day. Maria puts her hair up, and wears a better-fitting set of clothes today.

"Remember that flying recorder that looks like a mosquito?" I do not tell her where else it has been. "The one we left on the beach? Matthew Park went to pick it up, so he can review the recordings afterwards and know what happens. We call this a *surveil*. After that, he can tell me just enough of what happens for me to change the rest."

She nods. "*Sí…*"

"The bug is a little bit naughty of me." I say. "It is from the 2030s, very fine. Only a time-active would know it for what it is, someone who would not mistake the bug for a mosquito. We know it is either Will or Rachel, either time-active or not. He knows the bug is there. He knows what it looks like."

It dawns on her.

"He took your very fine flying bug. That's how you know it's him." She says. She looks ready to offer me a cigarillo. "Very clever, Gabriel."

So...Will has a motive. A reason to kill me. Even if I don't know what it is just yet, it must be there. And it all fits together: His cover-ups. His twinnings. His mysterious errands. His being short on time even when Alison and María and Uncle Jerry are skipping as normal.

There is no nexus that Easter. There never was. There are only two of us short on time. Him... and me.

"But first," I say, "we have business to attend to." I hand her ten crisp bills from 1951 and 1961.

"Gabriel," she says, "I can't..."

"Take it." I say. "Use it to make yourself a little nest egg with compound interest. Pay me back in 2014."

She doesn't need asking twice, and snaps the bills from my hand.

"Interest is theft." They slap against her palm as she counts them again. "But I can buy some cigars and resell them in twenty years when they are ripe, no?"

I chuckle.

"Buy Cubans."

"Why?" she asks. "I thought you were Mexican?"

"Trust me on this one."

She pockets the money, and grins a lopsided smirk at me. "I know a good cigar when I smell one, *señor*."

I leave the key on the desk. She picks up her bags, hands them to me, and extends a callused hand. I put my own palm in it, and feel her squeeze. The last thing I see before I close my eyes is her determined stare into the horizon, as if she would cross it in a heartbeat.

We land in a heap on top of Black Hill, the shock of the mountain coming up to meet me through my rolling shoulder. María has pushed herself as far as she can go, and she missed a little bit. Fortunately, it is dark and the stars are out, and no one is close enough to see... still, I wait a moment for Park, or worse, Will, to show and wrap us up in our clean-up. María's bags slump down and she practically folds into me.

"'m...sleepy..." she lisps.

"María." I shake her a little. "María! Wake up, I am not carrying you down the hill and it would take a lot of 'splaining if I walked into a hotel with an unconscious woman anyway..."

She tries to slide to the ground. Her skin is warm and clammy, her shirt soaked through with sweat. I give her another shake, and she murmurs her annoyance. It reminds me a little of Rachel. Crazy Spaniard!

I go down to my knees, letting her down on her back in the flat rock and the grasses of the top of the hill. As her shoulder hits a rock, her eyes spring open, bloodshot enough I can see even in the moonlight.

"I'm awake!" she shouts, rising up on her elbows. "I'm awake."

"At ease, soldier," I joke. "*Ay carumba* and I thought my wife was crazy! Do you know when we are?"

She looks around. "No..." Her eyes harden behind her clear exhaustion; her body stiffens, trying to gather up what energy she still has with tension. "Before...1987."

"Well, come on, Pirio Sanchez." I say. "Can you walk…?"

We make our way back down the hill, slowly, María hanging on me, stumbling along like she's drunk. And me with all four of our bags in my other hand. When you skip as far as you can, you start doing things like this… you miss your mark, you lose your bearings, and if you come out the other side, you just want to sleep for days. Pirio Sanchez is famous for doing it, the time-active version of a marathon runner. Once, at rank six, she crosses the Roman Empire in eight days. *Including* the Byzantines.

When we make it into the city, she's mostly just exhausted. She's pulled out of her comrade's arms and is insisting she's ready to march five hundred miles. She really is like Rachel. It's about 8:30 at night on June 3, 1977. *Madre de Diós* do I have an amnesiac skip prodigy on my hands? She fired off nearly two decades in a go, unassisted. I start wondering what rank she is. I thought she was below me, but people that good tend to populate the upper ranks, your eights and nines and tens and elevens.

She naps for an hour after we check into the Chinese-run motel. Somehow, we are in the same room again. Maybe it is the first room they let. No, it is the middle of summer, there are cars in the parking lot, that can't be. Maybe it is just coincidence.

I don't like coincidences.

When she wakes, we have a late dinner from Cam's Chinese where that nice pizza place will be in my time. Already, things look very different. Or, rather, we look very different. A *Mexicano* and his mistress, that is not so unusual to them. But María's straight black hair without curls, her bell-bottom jeans with their tight fit up top, my nice shirt…Morro Bay in the 1970s is a town of *gringo*s, and we look out of place in half a dozen little ways. Something I don't really want to think about.

In the end, we retreat to the hotel room to finish the bottle of Scotch. It could be 1977 or 1992. My guns in their holsters hang by the door. The bags, briefcase, and backpack are all in a heap in the corner. María sits on the end of the bed, her hair let down, and I sit in the chair by the desk. Her hair is surprisingly long, but I have only seen it up or falling out of the bun she keeps it in. It is not perfectly kept like Rachel's, there are frizzes and split ends, but then, she is not that kind of woman.

"So," I say, filling her coffee cup halfway, "why did you try to fling the both of us out into time?"

I say it with a joke in my voice, but with the hard look in my eye. María Ortega is of course unruffled. She shrugs, and meets my gaze with her own.

"I wanted to know." she says, raising the cup to her mouth. Her lips curl around the rim, and she holds it up. "To your health."

"To yours." I toast. We drink. The whiskey is warm down my gullet.

"I wanted to know how far I could go," she says, "in case one day I need to go that far. Or farther. I need to know how strong I am, so I know who's stronger than me…"

She crosses her legs at me. It is hard not to notice how deliciously tight the 2000s made women's jeans.

"…and who's not." The thunderbolt again, as her legs tense. I can see, even under the jeans, the muscles like steel cords.

"You could have killed us both trying to find out." I said.

"You seemed pretty sure of yourself hopping around yesterday." she says. She opens her mouth as if to say more, but then seems unsure how to proceed. It is a look that I have grown used to not seeing…she has in the last few days become more sure, come more into herself. I can see it in the quiet confidence of her walk, still wary, but aware, an animal that knows what it's about.

Right now, she looks like the little lost time traveler I met… *a diós mio*, only three days ago. It is a look that I can feel in my hip pocket.

"I know my limits," I say.

This time, she fills my coffee cup.

"You're getting there," she says, soldier to soldier and comrade to comrade. I nod, and let more whiskey warm my throat. "You are always the strong detective man, aren't you? Always the rock for others."

Her eyes are warm and smiling. It looks good on her.

"The one piece of wood floating in a wide sea." I quote.

"But you are the client *and* the detective this time, yes?" she says. "This time it's your feelings that are washing over."

My left thumb is rubbing against the warm gold of my wedding band. I try to remember the last time I felt Rachel's skin against mine, and suddenly need more whiskey. I am starting to feel it, mostly from the priming of the beer with dinner.

"You do so much to help others," she continues, "a *caballero* good and true. I'm just saying, I understand."

Her finger traces around the lip of her mug. "One cannot be a soldier all the time either."

"I don't have time to not be a detective." I say.

"You have all the time in the world," she points out, prodding me with her bare foot, "you're a time machine."

"Gotta go sometime." I muse philosophically. Now I am tracing my mug with my fingers. Why can't I stop thinking about fingers? "Even if I scoop up my wife and run off to the 2030s, I have a date with destiny."

"That again." María takes a pettish drink, looks in her mug, and holds it out. She says '*gracias*, Gabriel' when I fill us up, then continues. "Don't you get tired of running from appointment to appointment? Don't you ever wonder if you have any choice at all?"

"I'm a detective, motive is my business." I say. María just grins at me, and leans in.

"Not business," she says, "choice. If what will be, will be, what about us? Am I just acting out my part or do I have free will?"

"My mother would whip me if I said anything but free will." I say. Our hands with their mugs of Johnnie Walker Black are hanging between our legs.

"But you act like you are only following God's foreordained plan." she says. "You act like a Calvinist heretic. You are told you are here, you go here, you're told you're there, you go there."

"I have my duties," I tell her, leaning in, "but I also have choice."

"Prove it." Her voice is thick, with the alcohol or something else. "Prove to me you're more than just a puppet to some historical force of will."

Our lips form a seal before the thought has completely wound through my brain. It does not make it, because my brain lights up at the taste of her lips, the faint smell of tobacco that clings to her, the lightning bolt between us. Her mouth is tense with surprise, then relaxes, still alive and aware but welcoming, inviting, drawing me farther in.

We lean in farther, her arm wrapping around mine, her hand gripping my shoulder. My hand comes up and brushes her cheek. I am suddenly aware of the alcohol, and how my other hand is occupied, and we break the kiss.

I turn back and set my mug down on the desk, taking María's as she passes it to me. There is enough time in there for me to start thinking again, and when María leans in to kiss me more, I hold her gently by her shoulder.

"No." I say. "I'm sorry."

My thumb is back to rubbing against the gold on my finger. I screw my eyes shut and turn away, feeling the need pulsing in my slacks. *Madre de Diós*, how long has it been? A little more than a week, as far as Rachel is concerned, but the body has its own timeline and its own rhythm. And my body is telling me how overdue I am.

And this woman, she is strong, but vulnerable. Like Francesca. Like Rachel. Like any woman I've ever admired.

I feel a warm hand on my shoulder again. So warm, it burns.

"She's not even born yet." María says. "Things happen."

She does not have to finish: things happen on the battlefield. I wonder how many tomorrowless nights she's spent tumbling with fellow *compañeros*? I wonder how many of them were still alive the next night, and how many lay dead in ditches, alleys, streets, mud and cobbles. Yes, I know where she's coming from. We are alive now. And I won't be alive tomorrow.

Better, then, to die Rachel McCoy's husband and not María Ortega's lover. She deserves a good man. I reach up and squeeze the hand at my left shoulder. It would be glorious. It would be sinful. It would be gloriously sinful.

"Things don't have to happen." I open my eyes and meet María's. It hurts, a pain I cannot describe, but which any man who has disappointed a woman will know. "I have a choice."

Her smile is sad. She sits back down on the bed, her legs still loose and her hands on her open knees.

"It's about Rachel, isn't it?" she says.

"It is not because you aren't..." I have to choose words carefully. "...very, *very* attractive, *señorita*."

For once, María is actually charmed by this.

"But I can't do that to her." I say. "I love my wife. I can't do that to her."

"Yesterday, you thought she might be your murderer." María says. Her voice is disappointed, but resilient. A good sleep will mend her.

"And you helped me prove she wasn't." I reminded her. "Only a time-active would have recognized those bugs, and only Will knew they were there. Will also makes more logical sense, as he would have time to put on gloves and so on. *Ipso facto* not Rachel."

She looks away. She is a soldier, she does not want anyone to see her hurting.

"The *one* man who's faithful to his wife..." she mutters.

I want to sit on the bed next to her, put my arm around her narrow shoulders, hug her and tell her it's all right. But I cannot. It would not end there.

"I'm going to take a walk." I say. "I will be back in around ten minutes."

We don't say why, or for whom. Neither one of us wants to insult the other's *machismo*.

It is good to feel the chill on my cheeks and the warmth in my legs. I walk down to Happy Jack's, as everything else in town is closed promptly at ten. The pizza place where Cam's now stands is open until 11:30, but it's 1977 and they haven't even built the Burger King yet, much less Sabetta's. The little ways that the town is different, with different shops and different clothes, starts to hit me. It's funny...I came from the 1930s, but now 2014 feels like home.

2014 feels like home because Rachel is there. And because Amá is there.

I'm gone a bit longer than ten minutes, lingering over my beer. I have met the former owner once, just before the sale. By then, she was pinched and bottle-blonde. Now, she is a little tired, but friendly and vivacious. I like her.

I am just tipsy enough that skipping would be a very, very bad idea, so I walk back to the motel. When I turn the key, María is already asleep, turned toward the wall, away from me. I brush my teeth and take a cold shower, and turn out the light after I put on some pajamas. In the darkness, I spend a long time contemplating the warm, breathing body next to mine, and how I could have her if I only reach over. How she would turn towards me, and her body would melt into mine. How close she is, and how willing, and how she would never mention it…only soldiers in the dark before the harsh light of day. How her breasts would feel against my chest, and her thighs against mine.

I sleep in the chair.

The next morning, we share our space without talking, and keep careful of one another. She dresses in relaxed jeans and a much less tight top than yesterday. Hopefully, if María is not too tired, we can make it all the way to that day in July of 1958. By my estimate, she skipped nearly twenty years all together yesterday.

"Gabriel." she says as I am turning the key in the lock. I meet her eyes, and my stomach gets ready to drop. Then she says, in Spanish: "you're a good man."

She smiles at me. I smile at her. And that's all that needs to be said.

We grab breakfast, and make the march up the hill. Rachel and I are in a habit of racing each other to the top. As much as I enjoy that, it's nice to take it at a leisurely stroll with someone.

"Think you can make ten years, María?" I ask, once we have reached the copse.

"What, 1967?" she considers it. "I think I can do that."

She hands me her two shopping bags, stuffed with the ransom of two separate hotels.

"And *not* fall asleep on my arm when you do?" I check, taking them.

"Probably not." she has the hint of a smile. She holds out her free hand, I hold out mine.

It's a late summer day in 1967 when we arrive, and María does indeed lean on my arm…but only for a few minutes while she catches her breath.

"Why aren't you out of breath when *you* skip?" she demands.

"I only skip a little ways at a time," I tell her, "you're skipping decades at a stretch."

"Lazy-ass Mexican."

"Crazy-ass Spaniard."

"So how far can *you* go?"

"I can get us to 1958 from here."

"Whenever you're ready, *señor.*"

And thus we left the Summer of Love the *gringos* rhapsodize so much about.

1958 takes a bit out of me. I feel winded, and it's my turn to lean on María for a moment. I really need to practice my distance skipping more. She does not comment, and wordlessly hands me back my briefcase when I am ready. I take out the card with the address on it, and hand it to María. We start walking back down the hill.

It's high July, the 22nd, and the sun is warm but not too warm in that way Morro Bay has in the summer. Perfect weather for kayaking in the bay or running along the beach.

"Promise you'll come by every so often?" María asks as we turn onto Main Street.

"Only if you come by and visit me." I say. "I don't hang around in this century very much."

She nods. "Too many memories."

"Too many memories." I agree.

It's such a nice day…tired as I am, my body calls me to the shore, to stretch and run and play ball. But we have an appointment to keep.

As we walk, I eye María's hair. She has it up again, but something is nagging me about it. Something unrelated to the heat of the day or the desires of my body.

Finally, we come to the corner of Main Street and Morro Bay Boulevard, and I tug her to the left. The little barber shop looks entirely unchanged for fifty years' having melted from its face. It's one room the size of my living room in 2014, serviced by three barbers. They're good. I get my usual haircut and shave there at home.

I get one now, while we are waiting. We are definitely in the 1950s. The blue-eyed barber sneers at our presence until María explains that we are civilized Spaniards and not filthy Mexicans. He starts sneering again when he sees María's lack of a diamond ring. I say as little as possible, the *gringo* might know a Mexican accent if he heard one.

The card said 1:45. The arrogant young man takes from 1:22 to 1:52 to trim and shave me. No one enters, least of all María's long-lost twin sister.

I pay the man with an apologetic twenty from 1951, which he happily changes.

"Nobody?" I ask as we walk out.

"There was a young *inglés* who walked in, but when he saw us he turned around and went away," María reports. "Short, blond, early 20s. Limp on his left foot."

"Probably GI." I reply. María looks disappointed. "I wasn't expecting it to be so easy. Why would a woman in 1958 have an appointment at a men's barbershop?"

I look at her hair again, the thick strands falling into place.

"And you haven't had your hair cut recently." I explain, as if I did not just now figure this out. "Still, I was hoping to see your friend or your boyfriend or something. We are going to have to do this the hard way."

We spend most of the afternoon shopping, along with a late lunch of sandwiches and soup. I acquire a pair of slacks and a fedora and fit in immediately. María presents a special problem. If I had my truck, I would just put her in a wig and a hat, but as the truck is fifty-six years away, we must improvise. Still, she passes for a local in her new glasses and little French hat and pale rose sundress. As we are passing the block where 2Dogs, Cam's Chinese, and Rachel's favorite bookstore will one day stand, her ears prick up.

"Do you hear it?" She asks.

I strain my ears...yes...sounds like Amá's guitarwork.

We listen, and follow our footsteps, and find the guitarist sitting in front of a drugstore that will one day be an empty field. He is a tall spare *indio* in a floppy cap, busking for his supper with his great Army rucksack and his hard-back guitar case that is open for business. His fingers are not as deft as Amá's, but no one's fingers are as deft as Amá's. It is still the same piece; it is still "Bolero Mallorquin." And it is still absolutely beautiful.

As the nylon threads hum and the man's fingers dance, María is enraptured. The lines disappear from her face, the smoke and gunpowder and the regrets she cannot remember…and it is like she is seventeen again. She has the look on her face like Rachel while she is mudding or carrying the ball: the serenity, the true poise. Rachel looks like a little girl in those moments.

It is still on her face as the last notes die away in the warm sunshine.

"*Gracias, señor*." she says, all breathless pleasure. "Bolero Mallorquin, *si*?"

"*Si*." He says, scrutinizing her accent. "You play?"

Now shadows are coming back to María's face.

"No, I'm sad to say." she says. "I never had the opportunity. But I know good playing when I hear it. What are you called?"

He tells us. I keep my face very carefully blank.

"Do you have a record?"

The tall spare *indio* laughs, his floppy hat bouncing.

"No, *señorita*, no. Do you think I can afford to record an album when I am busy begging on the street?"

Without conscious thought, without even thinking, María takes out three 1951 hundreds, and lays them in front of the busker.

"Record it, *señor*." she says. "The world has too much war and oppression and all manner of capitalist coercion in it. And not nearly enough beauty."

He stares at the money in his guitar case.

"*G-gracias…la señora*." he manages. He offers María some of his tobacco, and they roll and smoke. He plays us a few more pieces, all of them beautiful and raw with a young man's playing, before apologizing as he must catch the train to Los Angeles. In two years, he will record Amá's favorite album there.

María looks like a cat who has just eaten the canary as we watch him turn the corner.

"When the revolution comes," she swears, "I will dance to his guitar."

"*¡Viva la Revolución!*" I pump my fist. "But I am supposed to tell you not to waste money like that."

"The People are the best investment." She says, with the conviction of a Carmelite.

I have known many, many time-actives. Some spent their first dollars betting on horses, or fights, or on stock tips or real estate or art. Some turn to financiers, some turn to banks, some turn to their own knowledge of something that becomes more valuable over the years. It says a lot about a man, how he bootstraps: how, given the workings of time and compound interest, he chooses to build his fortune.

I have known exactly two time-actives who spent their first dollars on people. And I smile to remember what became of Juana and the gold.

I just nod to María. "*Sí.*"

"But if it will save your sensibilities, I will purchase some cigars too." she grins.

"Try jewelry to start with. The gold and diamonds can always be sold."

"I will look like a *bourgeois* daughter!" she complains.

"And cigars are less *bourgeois*?" I note. "Besides, you can hide them on your person so they do not offend your delicate sensibilities."

We pass a *gringo* couple, him in his hat and she in her dress, the image of the white-picket fence family. His eyes narrow at us, and she pulls closer to him. Such people as us adulterers do not walk around in daylight.

"If I wear one ring," she says, "at least the *ingléses* will not look at us like this."

It is a very different María in the jeweler's. There is only calm appraisal, as a quartermaster would assess the worth of his boots and bayonets. She chooses logically, rationally, a necklace, two bracelets, sets of earrings, and a ring.

I know that ring.

One day, it will be Rachel's engagement ring.

María is right, too, it looks out-of-place on her finger. But there it stays for now, "to replace the one that fell down the sink." Other than the ring and the thin little necklace, María pockets the rest in her shopping bag. By now, it is almost five o'clock, unthinkably late in Morro Bay, and we close out the jeweler.

"Time to do this the hard way," I say, as we stand on the corner of Main Street and Harbor Street. Happy Jack's stands open before us, the name written out on the sign like it's written out on the matchbook in my briefcase.

I am certain that, at some point tonight, María Ortega will appear. She will get the card, probably from the blondie GI, and collect the matchbook. I did not count the matches she threw away in the Deep Dark, but it's not the whole book. María would have lit at least one cigarillo while in the bar.

In the 1950s, Happy Jack's has already acquired the aged, well-worn patina of an institution. There is an easy companionship along the length of the bar, the casual way ties are loosened, shoulders hang free, cigarettes glow affably, and smiles are soft.

I grin. Anyone who is not a regular will stick out like a sore thumb.

We approach the bar, and as I am ordering my on-the-job ginger ale, I feel my hackles come up. María tugs my sleeve and nods towards the back of the bar, towards the bathroom. Our limping GI is just disappearing into the men's.

"Excuse me," I say, hustling towards the men's room myself.

A quick search of the men's room confirms it: the limping GI is time-active. There's not a trace of him. I curse, empty my bladder, and walk back to María at the bar.

Along the way, I feel the hackles go up again. Ah, but now I know *why*.

"...what is this grin?" María asks, looking at me quizzically. I take up my drink, and she takes up hers.

"Come with me." I offer her my arm. She takes it, the ring glinting in the low light.

The bar extends along the whole of the room, along one wall. The front third of the room is partly separated from the more private lounge area in the back. Along the wall opposite the bar, in the corner, there is a table. María and I approach this table.

María's *joven* is wearing the dress I first met her in, the red sack-cut. She has her hair in a bun and is drinking some kind of hard liquor that's amber in color. She sat with her back to the corner, so that no one can sneak up on her. María slides in beside María, and I sit opposite her.

There is a look on the younger María's face that I have never seen. She is guarded, yes, that is her character…but this María is downright predatory. She is not only assessing danger, she is assessing prey. This alley cat has sharp claws and is ready to use them.

"Who are you?" she asks, in flawless English.

"*Me llamo Gabriel Caballero y Gutiérrez.*" I say.

Several things happen in the next five seconds.

María's eyes go wide, as if God had ripped the roof off the building and reached out for her. The shock passes and seemingly every muscle of her body tenses. With lightning-quick training, her left arm snakes down under the table.

And with lightning-quick reflexes, the ring glints as María's left hand grips her *joven*'s wrist.

She speaks quietly and with authority, in what I think is Catalan. To me it sounds like a drunken Frenchwoman speaking Spanish, but what do I know, I'm from Jalisco. I can make out "no," "savior," and "attack." María takes off her glasses and the hat, and both can see for themselves that they are identical, except for the color and cut of their dresses.

The María in the red dress, her eyes dart between her *vieja* and me. She does not relax. I force myself to relax, take a sip of my ginger ale in a whiskey tumbler.

"My *vieja* tells me you have taken care of her," she says, in careful Spanish, "that you saved her from a Free Will attack and solved her case and found her food and shelter and money. Why would you do this?"

"The People are the best investment." I say. María catches the smirk on her *vieja's* face.

"Why bring her to me?" she asks. "Why not to our *vieja?*"

"I looked. But I could not find the moment where your *vieja* would be. You are a slippery eel, *señorita* Ortega." I say. "We deduced your whenabouts here only with great difficulty."

She nods, calculating. She still has not relaxed. But her eyes dart around, as if expecting a series of quiet flashes and damn the drinkers and the Sixth Law.

"Can you help her?" I ask. She turns to her *vieja*, who lets go of her hand. Her eyes trace the movement of her *vieja's* left.

"What is that?" she asks.

"A wedding band." I tell her, in all truth. Both Marías give me startled eyes, an expression in stereo. The younger María looks over her *vieja* again.

"Yes, I think she can be helped." she said. "But this is all...very unbelievable. Can you prove it? It is very convenient that she cannot remember our protocol."

Slowly, I rise, and lean over the table. María digs herself deeper into the corner. Her *vieja* gives her a dirty look, and María leans forward again, her ear to my mouth and cupped hand.

"Francisco." I whisper. I can feel the muscles of her jaw working under my hand.

She sits back, watches me sit down. Both our hands are on the table.

"I believe you," she says, "now never utter that name in my presence again."

Her *vieja* looks at her quizzically. The María in red glances at her, then turns away. She is a soldier, she doesn't want anyone to see her hurt.

"I am sorry, María." I tell her. I turn to the María in the rose dress. "And I am sorry that you will need to remember something that is clearly quite painful."

She shakes her head.

"It's all right." she says. "My pain makes me the woman I am."

They smile at each other. I feel redundant.

"If that is all, *señorita*," I say, and quickly add, "and *señora*, I have something I must take care of back home."

"Where's home?" The María in red asks, raising one dark eyebrow.

"2014." I say. "Your *vieja* can tell you all about it. It's not like you have to worry about getting the details right, for once."

She nods. The María in rose gives me the curt nod of *compañeros*. Of comrades.

As I am about to leave the lounge area, one of the María's voices rises up one more time.

"Gabriel Caballero y Gutiérrez," she says, all in red, "I owe you a favor."

XI

April 19, 2014 – 2:00:33 PM

I still cannot work out what Will's motive is. Why now? How has he gone from one of my warmest friends to my killer? I do not think he is a *maricón* jealous of Rachel, I have not learned anything incriminating about him, and it's not like money is a problem among us. It is not a revenge fantasy nurtured after many years, the crime is too slapdash. So why kill me?

But before I can deal with Will, I have something more important to attend to.

My wife.

I make sure to wear the clothes I left 2014 in before I make the last skip back to that warm April day. I will spend my last twelve hours in this life with my wife and her sister and Amá. It is a good way to go.

I hop in the rental car and swing by the house. The Prius is gone, the girls must be doing something before the game. I drop off the backpack and shuffle things around in my briefcase. When I'm ready, I call Rachel.

"Hello, Gabriel." I cannot read her voice. Is she angry to hear from me? Glad?

"Rachel, *amor mio…*" I start. It is not difficult to read my voice.

Fuck it. I am dead in twelve hours. Make this count.

"I love you, Rachel." I tell her. "I love you more than words can tell. I love that you have a good heart and a strong head. I love that

you play rugby and baseball and love to race me to the liquor store
and then come home and do math problems or read big thick books
by the fire. I love that noise you make when you win. I love that I
never, ever, ever have to worry that you will do something criminal. I
know you are a big girl and it makes you embarrassed, but that is
crazy…it is one of the reasons I love you so much, your bigness! You
are a crazy redhead and I love you for it. Kick ass at the meet
today…you know I will be there for you."

I hope she isn't driving. I may have just caused a traffic accident
if she is.

"Gooch, what's got into you? You sound like you haven't seen
me for a week!"

She has no idea. I feel the bigness of my heart turn fragile, fall
back on itself like a zeppelin with a hole in it. It is almost a physical
pain, a chilling. My briefcase and my guns are suddenly so heavy…

"Do you have Amá with you?" I ask. It is not difficult to read my
voice.

"Yes, Amá's with us. She's grooving to her iPod." Rachel says.
"Gooch, what's wrong? Y'all all right?"

I force myself to smile at my cell phone.

"I'm fine, *amor mio*." I say. "See you at the meet."

I click the phone off. I want to find her, hold her, make her
understand how much she means to me, how much I'm going to
miss her.

But this, I realize bitterly, is why the Sixth Law is there. Now she
is suspicious, and if I lived long enough to skip again, she would not

stop until she either found the truth or left me for all my lies. All my abuse.

The Sixth Law protects us, too. From ourselves.

I come to a decision. It squares my shoulders and lifts my head like a shot of tequila. I head out the door, and climb in my rental. I stop first with my accountant, and pass him one of Morgan's cards. I make sure that Rachel will have all of the bootstrap money I have socked away, the 'inheritance from my father.' She will get that research trip to Britain she's always wanted.

I meet up with Officer Park, and tell him my suspicions. He blanches, then he turns florid. He does not have to swear vengeance; I can see it in his eyes. Detective Sergeant William Howe has abused his powers with the Temporal Security Bureau to murder a man who trusts him. Matthew Park will not stop until Will is dead.

I ask him to break the news to Rachel. To tell her that I am dead, even if it is not widespread knowledge, so that she does not need to live the half-life of wondering if I will come back. I make sure that he and Vivian will be there for her, if it is necessary.

"If?" he asks.

"If." I say. "Ask your *viejo* if you want more than that."

In short, I spend my time putting my affairs in order, warning all and sundry that I am "expecting some trouble."

The last thing I do before heading for the meet is to go down to Giovanni's Fish Market, and order a big bread bowl of their chowder and a bottle of Pacifico. I sit on their deck over the water on a beautiful sunny day, savoring my lunch, soaking up the just-right warmth of the sun, and watching the boats gliding through the crystal blue water. The soft wisps of cloud in the sky are playful and perfect.

A long way from a dirt farm in Belaños. A long way from that scared little boy hiding his baby sister under the woodpile when the *Cristeros* rode through town.

Then, I drive to San Luis Obispo.

The meet is in the usual place, the Damon-Garcia Sports Fields on the edge of town, near the airport. Apparently there was an early baseball game so it had to be later in the day than usual; rugby's usually at one. Even so, the families and friends and lovers of the women's rugby team are already setting up their coolers, chairs, towels. The locals are playing against the Oakland team, and half the cars in the lot are from out of town. I make my way to the white and blue fluttering at one end of the field.

Rachel's stretching and laughing with the petite black girl from New Orleans, LeShawna Thibodaux. They make quite a pair, on the field and off. LeShawna grabs the ball and takes off like greased lighting, while Rachel makes sure nothing and no one stands in her way.

"*Hola*, girls." I grin. "LeShawna, can I speak to my wife for a moment?"

She exchanges glances with Rachel, and finds some reason to be away in another knot of teammates.

Rachel is in her bike shorts and the long #4 jersey. In the short sleeves, you can see all the bruising, and the long scar Lightfoot left her, and the dark interlacings of her Celtic knot tattoo peeking out from under the left sleeve. She's almost flaunting the bruises the scrum machine gave her, her skin already glowing with strength and a light sweat.

I play amateur games, and was hoping to on Tuesday in fact. I make a good half-back. But my woman, she is a born lock.

"Y'all okay, Gabriel?" Talking to LeShawna has drawn out Rachel's drawl. "Your phone call spooked me."

I smile that cock-eyed smile.

"I'm here, aren't I?"

"A little surprised you're not out with a client," she says. My smile disappears.

"Rachel, this is about you. This is about you getting your try." I say. "I'm here for you. I haven't even put money on this one! The least you can do is not insult my honor."

"Amazing, though, what gets shoved aside when some pretty girl's husband fucks around." she says.

Did she just…?

"Is there something you want to tell me?" My voice is quiet, my fists are balling up, and my chest is hot.

"Alright, ladies!" The coach shouts. Rachel spins on her heel and marches off towards the gathering 7s.

"Play hard!" I shout after her. "Get your damn goal!"

"I'll just pretend they're you!" she replies, without even turning around.

I storm to where Amá and Debbie-Anne are sitting. They both have chairs, Amá because she is old and Debbie-Anne because she is lazy. I sit on the ground next to the cooler. No *caballero* sits while a lady stands.

"What are you so angry about?" Amá asks in the Spanish of our youth. "It's a warm day and your *gringa loca* is strutting her stuff."

"Tell you later." I take Amá's weathered hand and squeeze it.

"So, okay." Debbie-Anne says. "This doesn't look like soccer."

"It's not." I tell her. "It's rugby. Think of it as British football. SLO wants to get the ball over *there*, Oakland wants to get it over *there*, by carrying it or kicking it. The big difference is that they can't pass forward."

"But they're not wearing any protection!"

"No, they aren't." I pause. "You remember your sister's majors?"

"Yeah, math and history."

"History of the Celts." I note. "Well, think of Oakland as the Romans."

Debbie-Anne blanches as her sister strides across the field like Boudicca in a #4 jersey.

"So what's a try?"

"That's when someone carries the ball into the goal." I explain. "But Rachel plays #4 lock, and she hasn't got a try all season."

"Is that why she's been so riled up all day?" Debbie-Anne asks.

It's one reason, I suppose.

"Shh! It's starting."

The out-of-towners are given the first kickoff, and I start to narrate the game for Amá. After only a few minutes, I have nearly forgotten to be angry. I love this: telling Amá what Rachel is doing at the games. She used to listen to the radio broadcasts of the *fútbol* games in our youth, and then later to the American baseball games. Now her brother is her radio, and she can still howl and whoop and curse for happiness.

Today, of course, there is an extra poignancy for me. And an extra awareness. Debbie-Anne is unusually quiet, attentive, watching her sister slam into those black and Chinese girls from Oakland and get slammed into in turn.

From scrum to ruck to line-out, Rachel proves herself, tackling Oakland girls to pop the ball out to fleet-footed LeShawna, mauling like 180 pounds of solid cat, even getting a kick or two in to gain territory. But she still hasn't got her try. She still hasn't scored her point.

The turn for us Caballeros comes in the second half. Two of the Oakland girls tackle LeShawna at 22 yards, and rather than release the ball into play, she lets it fly off to the side. The referees call the touch, and four girls each line up at the 22 yard line, just outside knifing distance. On our side are Rachel and Big Kaitlin the locks, with one of the props between them. LeShawna is hanging around to one side of Rachel, ready to cross to the back if Rachel catches the ball. SLO's hooker jogs out to the ball, and picks it up…and while everyone is watching her, I think Debbie-Anne and I are the only ones who see Rachel and LeShawna's quick little exchange of gestures.

"What's she doing?" Debbie-Anne asks.

I feel my heart rising in my throat. You do not need to check tomorrow's scores to see what is going to happen now.

"Watch." I say, grinning like a wolf.

SLO's hooker tosses the ball, and it sings low, only ten or twelve feet off the ground. Everybody jumps…Oakland, SLO, the fans…everybody jumps. The middle girl from Oakland hops in the air, and her teammates run in to hold her up…as Rachel leaps straight up and stretches her bruised, scarred, tattooed arms, wrapping around the ball.

She feints a pass to LeShawna, who hares off like she's caught it. Eyes follow her just long enough for Rachel to start down the field, twenty-two yards, twenty-two long-limbed strides. The Oakland backs converge on her as LeShawna shouts orders in her New Orleans English, and joins two more of SLO's fastest to close the distance to Rachel.

Rachel lets out a primal yell that fills up the sky as she slams into Oakland's stocky Chinese fullback. Their left wing also catches her, but the little wisp of a girl barely matters in the scheme of things. Rachel cradles the ball to her chest and soldiers on. Two of Oakland's girls dangle from my woman but she is moving, *a diós mio* she is still moving forward!

LeShawna slams into Rachel from behind, and the maul is properly joined. Another little burst of speed…the goal line is only a few yards away…

The two fly-halves join the knot of women, now slowing the maul, now advancing. And still in the center I can see that crown of red hair, shoving forward. There is shouting, a force of will that you feel more than hear. Finally, at the one-yard line, the *puta* inside-center from Oakland slams into the knot, and pulls the whole maul down. Women collapse everywhere, but with a final heave, Rachel collapses forward, clawing half over the top of the women shoving her back like she was swimming to shore...

...and the ball comes to rest a hair past the goal line, Rachel's claws still buried in it.

We all surge to our feet, the point forcing an explosion of energy from the whole hometown side. No one is whooping and hollering louder than the Caballero clan, even Amá is hopping up and down for joy.

Play is halted to score the point, and Rachel holds up her trembling arms in victory, that all-over smile almost outshining the sun. She got her damn try.

"*¡Híjole! ¡Viva San Luis Obispo, cabrónes!*" I shout, after belting *el grito*. I know I am being the stereotype of the excitable Mexican, but I do not *care*.

"What are we shouting for?" Amá asks with coquettish politeness. I take great pleasure in telling Amá what just happened. And helping her to sit back down.

"Now do you believe me?" I ask Debbie-Anne. She's radiating all warmth and smiles, the way her sister radiates heat and power.

"I haven't seen her hit anybody that hard since they told her girls couldn't play on the football team!" Debbie-Anne says.

I chuckle, and open up another of the Cokes Debbie-Anne brought.

The game wraps up just after five, SLO carrying the day. Amá shouts a number of uncouth things in Jalisco Spanish to celebrate, Debbie-Anne and I settle for shouting ourselves hoarse. Oakland's players are good sports, and I catch sight of Rachel shaking hands with her counterpart, Oakland's #4 lock, but mostly she, Big Kaitlin and LeShawna hook up together and wander around congratulating teammates. I leave Amá in Debbie-Anne's care, and make my way down to the field.

"*¡Hola, la señora #4!*" I shout, grinning so hard it hurts. "The champion! The conqueror!"

Rachel turns to me, and her smile retreats a little.

"Let me buy the first drink, huh?" I say.

"The girls and I are headed to Spike's!" she shouts back. "Coach wants to twist my ear about my try! But I'll be home by eight! Can you take Amá and Debbie-Anne home?"

My heart falls out of me. I open my mouth one or two times, but I have two horns that I am grappling: either I must lie to her, or I must tell her the truth. I can't do either. What am I going to say? "This is our last night together?" No. There are too many questions. But she is so happy and tired and wonderfully *alive* in every way that I cannot bring myself to lie to her. Not right now. Not while she's happy.

"Drive safe!" I tell her, at last. It rings hollow in my ears, but some of the smile comes back, and she disappears into the retreating white and blue of SLO Women's Rugby.

Amá and Debbie-Anne talk excitedly of their homegrown Boudicca, with yours truly translating freely. By the time we hit the city limits, I am no longer necessary, and they are in the backseat communicating in a women's language all their own, composed of squeals and touches and the hums of phrases.

My meeting with Will, tonight in Legends, comes back to me. I can feel the desire to go Nuremburg like I can feel the wind from the road and the unfamiliar seat. So much to fix...Debbie-Anne's broken wrist, not telling Rachel from the beginning, not telling her it is our last night together, Elliot, Juana and the gold, my death...

I feel dizzy. The girls are still talking. I miss Rachel very deeply, the feelings coming over me like waves. Maybe this is what Will means about it driving you crazy. About knowing. I know I cannot run and fetch her, I know I will not see her after tomorrow.

No, I tell myself. That is the one thing I do *not* know, that I cannot know, until it happens. Only in that ignorance do I have any freedom to change things. I cannot change what I know, but I can change what is unknown.

As we pull into town, I gather my wits. I take the girls out to Chapala Market back home for a nice round of enchiladas, and chat excitedly with the owner about Rachel's win. He offers his congratulations and looks forward to giving them in person the next time Rachel and I come out.

After dinner, we head home. Amá heads around the back to catch the Mexican news and yell at the *Cámara de Diputados*, while Debbie-Anne and I sip beers in the living room and catch up. She is not Rachel, but she is family, dammit. A few times, she opens her mouth like she wants to speak, then takes a sip and talks about something else. Something seems off, something I can't put my finger on, and I put it down to embarrassment over what happened today.

Finally, the door flings open, and Rachel is standing there, still grinning and still dressed in her 'battle fatigues.'

"Well," Debbie-Anne drawls, "if it ain't Queen Boudicca herself."

Rachel just grins, strides over, and wraps her arms around her sister. Debbie-Anne manages an 'eep!' but doesn't flinch away, no matter how caked with mud her sister still is. I chuckle and down the dregs of my Pacifico.

When she lets Debbie-Anne breathe again, she turns to me.

"Queen Boudicca is victorious!" she announces. "And *sober!* But now I'm home and I ain't drivin, so that needs fixin'! I seem to recall somebody offered the first drink?"

"After that play," I say, my heart bursting in my chest, "I think I am offering *every* drink."

Debbie-Anne catches her sister's eye, and that incomprehensible communication goes on again. I swear on my mother's grave, the McCoys are mind readers. Rachel's mother and older sister do the same thing.

"I think I'll stay home for this one." Debbie-Anne says at last.

I shrug, and gesture to the open door. "After you, *señora.*"

We walk down to the corner of Main Street and Harbor Street, about five blocks. Now, what was once Happy Jack's is the loud thumping Fuel Dock…but on the opposite corner, Legends is still the place for a quiet beer and a game of pool. And for a Saturday night, it *is* rather quiet…only the karate guys having a post-workout beer, and a *güey* trying to pick up a *chica* by beating her at pool. I suppose everyone is turning in early to go to church tomorrow.

Randy looks up at us from across the bar, and smiles.

"How was the game?" He asks as we walk in.

"I got my fuckin' try!" Rachel says, plastering her public grin on. Gettin' ready to interact proper. Randy looks confused, and Rachel launches into a rapidfire blow-by-blow while I translate from rugby-speak into terms Randy is likely to understand. Finally, he offers Rachel a high-five, which she gladly takes.

"And what'll you guys be having?"

"I'll have the black label, neat." I say. Then I remember the last time I drank it, and change my mind. "On the rocks, actually. And whatever this young lady will have."

She may play baseball and rugby and paint skate parks and give me a run for my money, but my woman still appreciates it when a real *caballero* treats her like a woman.

"Johnnie Walker Red, neat, if you please." she says. "Could use the warmth."

When our drinks appear, I am about to settle back on my bar stool for a leisurely sip when Rachel gets a glint in her eye.

"Fuckin' race ya." She says. We clink glasses, and down our drinks. We huff and puff a little at the first burn of the alcohol.

She shakes her head and lets out a long sigh. The alcohol is already touching her, and she has had a long day. After lots of talking or playing, Rachel can sometimes need time with a book or a workout. And she looks like she's getting close to needing one or the other.

"Race you another." she grins tiredly.

Or she might not care. Fine. I can go as long as she can.

"Randy!" I call. "Tequilas! Neat."

"On the rocks!" Rachel says. I give her a side glance. Now she is just *trying* to piss me off.

He brings our glasses. I pour the salt on, lay the lemon, clink glasses with Rachel, and down my shot. The salt and the lemon help keep it down. Rachel just smirks at me, her glass wrapped up in her hand up against her shoulder. The smirk is not a friendly smirk.

"What's wrong, hun?" she asks. "Can't hold your liquor?"

I furrow my brow at her, and we order the same again.

"This is the best of Belaños." I say. "I grew up with this."

We down our drinks.

"Then how come I'm taking it straight and you have to do the whole salt-and-lemon thing?"

"You're not drinking it straight," I point out, "it's got ice in it. *Ruins* the flavor."

"Oh like you can taste anything after all the other crap." she snaps at me.

I'm blinking from the about-face when she pipes up again.

"Whiskeys?" She asks, eying her empty shot glass. "I'm getting tired of so much Mexican bullshit."

To hell with it. I'm getting drunk and I die tomorrow.

"Rachel, you've been jumping down my throat every chance you get." I say. "What is the problem?"

"Problem?" she hisses. "There's no fuckin' problem."

"Then why are you always angry at me?" I say. "I come home, I don't want my woman always yelling at me and won't say why!"

"Then maybe you married the wrong fuckin' woman." Rachel says. She looks ready to say more.

I signal Randy for two more whiskeys. "Rachel, what the hell?"

"You're always, always forgetting about things." she says. The tumblers are by our elbows. Before she starts, I pluck mine up and take a sip. The previous…however many drinks…are hitting me. "Sometimes I wonder if you remember what *year* it is. Like Thursday night. I didn't want to with Will coming over on Good Friday, but Debbie-Anne wanted that damn potluck and you were supposed to be with us, remember? Our dinner with Debbie-Anne, who's come out just to see us! And you *stood us up!*"

"Is *that* what this is about?" I ask, scrambling to find a lie to cover-

"No, Gooch, that isn't what this is about." she lies. "Yes, it hurt a little that you forgot your *sister-in-law* and your *wife*. …actually, I lie, it hurts a lot. But I'm mostly wondering *why* you stood us up."

Rachel downs the rest of her tumbler in one gulp. She slams it on the bar with enough force to make Randy understand "another, or I will end you." The karate guys look up, then quickly go back to their beers.

"And then that *call* this afternoon…" Rachel says. "That's not like you. You don't just call and say those things. And I ask myself, is he guilty? Is that it? Is he feeling guilty? What could he be feeling guilty about?"

She doesn't bother sipping this one either, she just knocks it straight back like it was a shotglass and not a tumbler. I knock back my own.

"You think too much." I tell her. "That big brain of yours is crowding out your eyes and ears."

"Goddammit Gabriel if you're cheating on me I will fucking *kill you!*" Rachel's up on her feet now, leaning over me, trying to intimidate me, energy tingling through her. She goads me on: "Go ahead! Deny it! G'won!"

Something snaps in my brain, and I surge to my feet, craning up into her and getting all up in her business.

"You think I don't see temptation?" I shout, gesturing wildly with glass in hand. "Huh? I see these women when they are scared and alone and adrift. Their children are missing, their husband is gone, or he might be cheating on them. The world is all wrong! And they look to me to put it right, to be the knight in white armor! Yes, they offer. And yes, some of them are beautiful, and some of them are even redheads. And I always turn them down. I am a Caballero, *chingao*, we have our *honor!*"

I take a moment to breathe. My breath is hard as straight tequila. Rachel's face is about three inches away from mine, but I can barely see for the tequila anger.

"I am faithful to my wife and I am a professional, and you can ask anyone. I'm a *caballero* good and true. I earn my keep and put bread on my family's table, I treat my women with respect, I never strike you *no matter what your sister thinks* and I don't lose my head on the job, least of all over some skirt."

"So who was that little wetback bitch you were checking into the Sands yesterday?" She asks. I lean back, in shock. Rachel at least has enough shame to keep her voice down this time.

It is not enough. My arms and legs all feel cold. This is *dangerous* anger.

"What did you just say?" I ask. "*What* did you call her?"

"A little bitch." Rachel sneers. But she does not move in. She does not loom.

"No, I'm very certain there was another word in there." I say.

"You're getting angry over one little word?" she demands.

"Yes." I say, very quietly. "Yes, I am."

She has no idea how many times I have defended her against the one little word 'mundane.' How many sneers or side-glances have come along with it, as if I married an *indio*'s half-breed daughter and all the other *blancos* and *blancas* can't decide whether to pity, mock, or excommunicate me. I won't stand for her to sully her honor and to insult me by tossing such words around herself.

"You tell me and I'll apologize."

Rachel's offering terms. If I were calm enough, I'd notice that's a good thing.

"She was a client." I say. "One who lost her memory, and did not know where she lived. I checked her in last night while I ran a records search. I took her home this afternoon."

I take out the billfold of 90s and 80s bills and smack it on the bar top.

"And I got paid." I tell her. "It's going in the Britain fund."

Well, most of it is going back to the money men. Morgan will make sure the Britain fund is well-stocked.

"Now." I say. "I think you owe a fucking apology."

"Sorry." she sneers. With her running this hot, it's as much as I'm getting. "An amnesiac client? *Really?* I went to Ole Miss, Gabriel, not some third-rate community college. I'm not *dumb*. Besides, Debbie-Anne tells me she's such a tiny little thing..."

Rachel hunches down over the bar.

"...Gabriel, look me in the eye." she finally declares. I meet her gaze, look into those honey-brown eyes. "Are you cheating on me?"

I think of María, of our stolen kiss, of the things that happen that don't have to happen. I think of her words, and of my choice.

The answer is instant.

"No." I say. "I never have. I never will."

She has seen me lie so often, lies sound like truth to her. But, for once, she believes me when I tell her the truth.

"And I'm sorry I missed Debbie-Anne's potluck." I say. "That was disrespectful to you and to Debbie-Anne. You know how I love you both. You know I don't want to hurt you."

"I just wish we were..." Her voice is starting to go. "...more important to you..."

"Rachel." I say. "You are the most important person in my life. If I were going to die tomorrow, all I would worry about is how you would go on."

And it's all true. Her toughness starts to crack. She would never forgive me for letting her look weak in public.

"Come on, Lucy, come on." I say, wrapping my arm around her. She takes a hard breath, holding in the sobs. Randy looks at us curiously, I mouth 'tomorrow' and escort my wife out the door.

She stands and trembles in my arms, a great big marble statue of womanhood with her bronze locks shivering. I hug her, and stroke my hand down the back of her neck, where her shirt is just open enough for my hand. I feel the sobs she chokes down. And I feel her wrap her arms around me and squeeze tight. I squeeze tighter. We almost kill each other.

All is well.

"I need t'run." she says. "Gotta move. Race you home?"

"Sober enough?" I ask. "We downed…"

"You downed four, I downed five." She holds up her open palm. She manages to crack a smile. "HA!"

"Race you to the liquor store." I tell her. "We'll see if we stay upright."

We get in place at the corner, I hold her back.

"Wait, wait." I look back and forth for the nonexistent cars. Morro Bay? 10:30 at night? Traffic? *Es imposible.* But she is too drunk to notice. I take off, and I can hear her laughing "oh, Gabriel, you *bastard!*"

I beat her to the liquor store. But she beats me home.

We have a couple of glasses of water at the breakfast bar, radiating heat, panting, rubbing up against each other. At one point, I think Debbie-Anne appeared at the top of the stairs. If she did, she was unusually smart and turned around and went straight back to the guest bedroom.

After the fourth glass, Rachel leans over and kisses me. So I kiss her right back.

Rachel's kisses are big and bold and strong and good, just like the rest of her. They're a challenge, to kiss her just as hard, to escalate, to take her in all her strength. Water or no water, my head is spinning, and I shove her back against the wall. I feel the thud, feel her moving, hear the wedding pictures rattle ominously. Rachel's hands are in my shirt front, and she tears the shirt open like tissue paper. We'll spend all morning picking up buttons, I'm sure. Her hands are exploring, invading, laying claim to all the scars and expanses of my body.

I pin her to the wall, and she purrs into my mouth, working her hips against mine. My hands are under her t-shirt, and we break the kiss. The honey-brown eyes flash something at me, something intense and passionate...and loving.

She tears my clothes off. I tear hers off. She drags me to the ground, I flip her over. We leave marks on each other with our teeth, our lips, Rachel's nails, my fingers. She has that all-over grin and the flush is spreading down her chest almost to her nipples. It's about as dark as her hair, and burns against the intricate knots of her tattoo that ties from her bicep over her left shoulder. The heat comes off her in waves.

I build up a rhythm, wrestling with her on the living room floor. I romance her, faster and faster, but always with rhythm. That's one stereotype that's true: We Mexicans *really do* have the best rhythm.

At least until our wives squeeze our asses with their claws sharp enough to leave ten narrow welts.

"Rachel..." I say, as I burst my seams. I cannot help it.

I screw my eyes shut, but it is far longer than a blink.

"MINE!" she announces to the sky. Her hips churn against mine, and I groan with her love. When I have control over my muscles again, I take hold of her neck with my teeth, right on the spot forming a hickey.

"Mine!" I hiss. That's enough. I feel Rachel's arms wrapping around me, enfolding me, her throat vibrating with her moan.

Afterward, we are laying naked on the living room floor, and I stroke her ribs.

"Yours." she burbles.

"Yours..." I murmur.

XII

April 20, 2014 – 12:12:12 AM

Like all the McCoy clan, Rachel could sleep through an earthquake.
So when she is good and deep, I carry her upstairs and lay her in bed,
tucking her in like a daughter. She will need to wash the sheets
tomorrow.

There's a lot she will need to do tomorrow.

While she slumbers, I go downstairs to my office and take out
some fresh sheets of paper. I could leave a message on her computer,
but love notes and last confessions should be written longhand. I
have always believed this.

In the letter, I tell her.

I tell her *everything*.

I tell her that Amá is my sister Francesca. That I was born in
1919, how we two and only we two dreamed of life beyond Belaños'
plaza and the local mission and the farm. How I raced after her that
night when she eloped, and how I got the *cabaceo*. I tell her about
Juana and the gold, about meeting *la Malinche*, about my time in the
2030s under Jessica's tutelage and about how I followed Lightfoot
across three decades. I tell her what I have done to protect people
like her from people like me, and why. I tell her about finding my
body, about my death, about who's responsible, and about María. I
tell her how much I love her, how much I have always loved her,
how crazy I am with love of her. I tell her not to breathe a word to
anyone, on my grave and on her honor and for sake of her life. I

leave Park's and several other names out. My death will shock her into silence if she does not know who to ask, but if I name names, curiosity will one day kill my Pandora.

In the end, I ask her to light a votive for me at the mission and pray to God and the Virgin Mary for a soul who will not have his last rites. It is only right.

This is the last piece of business I have in this life. I fold it up with the photo of me and *la Malinche*, taken on a beach in 1532, and put it in an envelope with her name on it. I leave it on the dining room table and hang the murder weapon in its place on the last peg by the door. I feed the chain-of-evidence card to the gas fire.

Everything has a surreal, dreamlike quality. The quietness and darkness of the house, the feel of the jeans and weighted jacket and handmade sweater and hiking boots that I will die in, the weight of my revolvers as I don the holsters. I feel like a puppet, like my will is not my own. Finally, I close the door and turn the key for the last time.

My papa told me a man's measure is in how he faces his death. Papa died of a bullet between his eyes, drunkenly shouting at the men on their horses as they rode up to liberate the farm. I am quiet, and my eyes are dry. I am the one with the guns now, and I am wearing my boots. My women are safe and provided for.

And I know that I die fighting.

I only regret that Rachel's copper hair will disappear under the black of a widow's shawl, and that there is not a child to hold her and bring her solace. A son, if I could ask God for such things. A boy to carry the Caballero name.

The way from my house to that stretch of beach is not too long, in the scheme of things. But it is somehow too long and too short, and no time travel is involved.

The moonlight is twinkling in sharp shards on the waters of the bay. The fog will roll in soon. But I can already see a dark figure standing in the middle of the beach, where in a few hours Will and I will crouch down and turn the body over.

I step over the creosote log and into my fate.

Will flicks his lighter open and lights the cherry on the edge of his Camel. He's ageless, well-built, with a nice, full smile...everything a proper time-active should be. Will's hair looks almost silver in the moonlight, but his eyes are shadowed. I don't have to see to know how wrinkled they are, how craggy.

"I knew it was you." I tell him.

"How'd you figure it out?" he asks.

"The nexus." I say. "Or, rather, the non-nexus. Jerry and Alison and everyone don't have any problems Bill-and-Tedding. Just you and me. And the scarf was never returned. ...rude of you to make me do it."

"It could have been a mundane." Will says. I bridle a little, but it feels distant.

"Look at our footprints." I say. "No one walked away from here. Last I checked, not even my wife can jump that far."

He considers this.

"Nice work." he says, ruefully.

"I'm guessing the twinning you had Alison clean up was you skipping back from this beach, no?" I ask. We are starting to circle one another. The moon is on me and off him. I'd like to make sure he's already regretting it when he skips.

"Alison talked?" he says. "That was damned disrespectful of her. Yes, he...I...was half mad. Crazy. Babbled everything to me, left me no room to...no room to maneuver. Can't get out of it, not without ripping cause and effect in half like a piece of paper. I have the whole script, Gooch, the *whole* thing, and now I have to say my lines. 'All the world's a stage, and men and women merely players. They have their exits and their entrances.'"

"'And one man in his time plays many parts.'" I finish. "Bombchild, brother, enforcer. Time-active, rank ten, Detective Sergeant. Friend, traitor, murderer."

Will giggles. It is very unsettling.

"And you know, I'm starting to get into it?" he says. "I'm *angry* at you...I want to tear you in *half*...for making me do this!"

"What did you grab at Rite-Aid on Friday morning?" I ask.

"Ask your *viejo*." he sneers. I can see the twist of his lip in the moonlight, the deep shadows around his eyes. The way his face is half-lit by the cherry on the end of his smoke.

Will does not want to tell me. He has something to hide, something he can keep in the shadows. I brush one hand past the unaccustomed weight in my jacket pocket. In the shadows of time, we can move and breathe and choose. In the shadows of time, we have free will. Will has been thrust into the light and now he is disintegrating under the heat.

"Do me a favor, *amigo*." I say. "I'm going to walk through this, you tell me where I'm wrong."

His eye is skeptical. I shrug.

"You know I'm dead in an hour." I say. "What do you have to lose?"

"A lot can happen in an hour. Or a moment." he says. I look around.

"You already cleared out my bug, I assume?"

For once, Will does not give me a lecture about using tech from twenty years in the future. But he takes my point.

"So your twin shows up Friday morning." I say. "Half mad, you said."

"Directly into my bedroom." Will replies. "Hell of a wakeup call."

"That explains why we did not see your 'visitor' on the stakeout. So, he tells you everything or almost everything you do in the next few days. You come get me, and take me to see the body. You take me before I am fully rested so I do not think to do the obvious thing and skip down here, now. You do a very good job covering your tracks...how many of your cigarettes did we pick up?"

"Three." He says.

"Park and Morgan show up. Park scares you. He came earlier than you expected, while you were in the middle of covering up the crime scene. So you smoke Camel after Camel and litter them around the body, so it looks like those three were just three more you smoke that morning. Same with us walking up and down to the tree line."

"That little cocksucker thinks he's hot shit because some loathesome little pimple of a town gave him a tin star." Will spits. "Nice to finally say that out loud."

"After that, you act like everything's normal…" I say. "…until the leftovers need to be eaten, anyway. You get a report of some drunks that were passing by the house when your *viejo* showed up. You have to call in Alison to cover it. What did you use to buy her off, anyway?"

"Knowledge of her extracurricular activities with homeless."

I laugh.

"That's funny, *señor*." I say. I clear my throat. "So you are skipping around as if you are not planning a friend's death. You must have been very happy when I kept you informed. When I told you about the bugs and about the surveil."

"And then I came here." he says. "I was always fated to come here, with you. We just never knew it. I'm carrying the bullet with your name on it. Innit funny? How we think we're in charge? How we think we have free will? How we think we have a *choice?*"

I think of María Ortega, and a little hotel room not too far from here, forty years away.

"And now we circle." I say. "And you strangle me."

Que será, será. What Will does, he does. Hell, he's even slid gloves on for the occasion, nice supple gloves he can still work a lighter in. I have a bit more freedom than that. I have more free will than that.

I choose my words very carefully.

"You made my wife a widow," I say, "you son of a *bitch!*"

The dance begins. I quick-draw the Colt and fire, but Will skips so fast the two flashes look like one. I have an afterimage blocking him out, on my right, as he wrestles me for the gun. I fire again, and skip to his left.

He's already behind me, and as Rachel's scarf cinches tight around my throat, my hand spasms. The Colt falls to the soft, cold sand. Instinctively, I reach up to tear the scarf away, dots forming at the edge of my vision, the blood in my head pounding.

I try to thrust my head back, bash his nose, but he's already in front of me, and the afterimages and the dots and the darkness are there. I grip at his arms, the ones yanking the ends of the scarf so hard I think he's going to snap my neck before I can choke.

My legs give way from underneath me, and I fall back into the sand. Will's straddled me, leaning forward, bracing himself on my shoulders, like a perverse afterimage of Rachel's climax only a few hours ago. The ankle-gun's too far away.

My coat pocket isn't.

A muscle spasm in my thumb flicks the switchblade open early, slicing the pocket lining out. I had Jerry drop in the pocket that morning, while I was waiting for María to emerge from her hotel. I draw it out, and bury it as deep as possible in Will's muscular thigh. He howls, but just draws the scarf tighter around my throat.

I go for a few more cuts, stabbing at his hips, his ribs, his side…hit the heart…remember the heart, Gabriel…between third and fourth…red…bleeding…a flash of light…is this the angels come to take me?

The red gives way to black.

XIII

April 20, 2014 – 4:09:00 AM

When I wake up, I am very, very surprised.

I imagine you are, too.

Consciousness comes slowly, and mostly in the form of awareness of cold, and a painful head, and darkness, and lapping water. At first, I think the whole world is shaking. Then I realize, I am the one who is shaking.

"Welcome back to the world of the living." María's voice...flawless English.

I scrabble up, and my head spins. I must hold it until the world stops spinning on me.

"Take it easy." she says, switching to her lisping Spanish. "You almost died."

"María...*Madre de Diós* what's happening?" I rasp, shivering and clutching my head.

"You were right, you know." she says. "About how to kill a time-active. Strangulation is far, far too slow. Plenty of people, time-active and not, have survived it. Will shouldn't have skipped away before he knew you were dead...waited at least fifteen minutes."

I look up, and see the cherry appear, lighting her face from below like a devil in the dark as she takes it from her mouth. María is wrapped up against the chilly fog that now obscures the moon, but she is barefoot. She is sitting on something, a long bundle.

"I can assure you I did not make the same mistake." She says.

"What...is that...?" I ask.

She grins wickedly in the moonlight.

"Ask your *viejo*." she says, shifting slightly.

She's perched on a body.

She's perched on *my* body.

"...you should *see* your *face* right now!" she grins. "Of course, you will need to switch clothes."

"*¿¡Que chingados chingado en el chingado que?!?*" I demand. Roughly translated: What the fucking fuck is that?

"It's your body." she says, mocking me. "The one they find on the beach in three hours."

"You killed my *viejo*?" I say, groggily coming to my feet. Maybe I can...

She hops off the body, leaving bare footprints in the sand.

"Take a closer look."

I don't have to. Now, I can see his clothes...the homespun shirt, the slacks Francesca sewed together...

...and now I know why they didn't find any scars on me. The color drains from my face.

"You killed my *joven*." I whisper. *Madre de Diós*...she has discorded me so far to hell that if I even *think* about skipping...I have heard stories. Better not to think about.

"You're not the only one who can pull tricks out of his pocket." María says, before taking another puff like a soldier.

"*¡Chingada de puta!*" I shout.

"*¿Puta?*" she says, exhaling a mouthful of smoke. "Me? I thought you would be thankful. I'm returning the favor I owe you *and* preserving your precious *que será, será* rule."

"Our rule...? So you are..." Free Will. I realize I have been dead wrong. About everything. ...almost everything.

"That's right." she says. "I did want to thank you."

"By destroying my worldline?" I demand.

"The problem with you people is you think you have the monopoly on honor." she says. "I will not let you kill me, Gabriel Caballero y Gutiérrez, but I take no man's help dishonestly. Now get *out* of your clothes."

"You are a madwoman!" I say. "Do you have any idea how many Laws of Time you've broken, how much of my life you've-"

"Gabriel!" she shouts. "According to you and your idea of history, there is a dead body on the beach tomorrow morning. Now, for sake of your precious First Law, it can either be this body..."

She flicks her half-spent cigarillo into the sand next to the dead man, just above high tide line, then turns back to me.

"...or yours." The look in her eyes is absolutely frightening, the dark, cold, calculating blackness of a rank twelve or a zealot. The look she had in the jeweler's, applied to killing. "I've already killed you once. If you turn me down, I have no problem doing it again."

I look from her to me, her to me. There is only one thing I can do.

"You could at least turn around."

She smiles, and the temperature on the beach drops ten degrees. "No."

And I realize she has me dead to rights. There is nothing I can do to stop her. My fate is in her hands. I curse and begin stripping.

"How do we not see your footprints?" I ask, tugging my sweater off.

She is unbuttoning the shirt on the body, with long, sure fingers. Like a lover.

"The body's below the high tide line. At 2:30, all evidence I was here is washed away." She runs one of her callused fingers down the dead man's chest, and I can feel an echo across my own skin. Or maybe it is only the fog.

She watches intently as I unbutton my jeans, even while her hands are unbuckling my *joven*'s pants.

"Except, of course, for half a footprint and half my cigarillo." She smiles. "Your beachcomber. You just have to flip the body into position and go home. I would walk below the tide line if I were you."

I shove my clothes at her, and she calmly hands me the clothes I haven't worn for twenty years. Or seventy, depending on how you count.

After I have dressed and stuffed the scarf around my neck in my shirt, she is just tying the last lace on the hiking boots. The body stares straight up into heaven and eternity.

"There." she says. "All ready. Oh, one last thing."

She reaches into her jacket and pulls out the Colt, then my Detective Special, handing them to me butts first. I spin the Colt and there are six empty clicks as I fire on María's chest. She puts one hand in her jacket pocket.

"I'm not stupid." she says, clinking the bullets together. "But I do have business elsewhere. This is it, Gabriel. Now we're square."

She steps back over the body, into the rising surf.

"Oh, and for the record?" she says. "Claiming to be married to a woman you kissed and then turned down is downright unmanly."

And in a quiet flash, she is gone.

I curse more, and turn my *joven* over onto the sand. I look and confirm: the scars are gone. This man never rides after Francesca that night, never falls from his horse, never meets Jessica or Park or Will.

Or Rachel.

I stand, and walk to the first eucalyptus tree, being careful to follow the footprints I have not laid yet. It takes me a long time to get home, while I let it sink in the full magnitude of what María has done to me.

Fucked me, that's what.

But why? Why, when I have done nothing to her? Because I will. "I won't let you kill me," isn't that what she said? So I am fated to kill María Ortega y Carerra, somewhere, somewhen.

Or I can choose otherwise.

I wish the liquor stores were open. Or that I could skip.

Because the discord, it hits you when you skip. Even just skipping across…well, discord is when you and the universe disagree on what happened. Step out of time, and now you can't step back in. Not really.

The universe and I have a very great disagreement on whether or not I'm dead.

But Rachel is warm and I am alive, and it is Easter, and yes, God, I am thankful for that.

When I arrive home, it is nearly dawn, and there are men shuffling in the porch light.

"...Gooch?" Park whispers.

I try to smile. I have no idea if I succeed.

"*Buenos dias, señores.*" I rasp. "Happy Easter."

I wonder if this is how Christ felt after rising on the third day. I decide probably not. Christ's head did not want to kill him.

"What happened?" Jerry asks.

"You were wrong." I tell them. "It was Will, not Rachel. Pre-destination motive: when I cut him, he skips back to have his *joven* take care of him, and reveals to his *joven* that he is not well upstairs and the events of his worldline. This makes Will start to go crazy...and try to kill me, the man he feels is responsible. Officer Park, I will have my official case notes to you by Wednesday."

They turn to Morgan, the oldest of us all, whose memory encompasses all that has happened here. He nods, what I say is true.

"And the body?" Vivian asks.

Morgan, Park and I look to one another. It slowly dawns on the others, and there is a hesitant drawing-away. I am a dead man walking, they think, only a matter of time before I must die on that beach. And among us, matters of time are very strict.

I do not correct their impressions.

"Go home." I say. "I have had a very long day, and all I want is to eat breakfast and then go to Mass with my wife and my sister."

One by one, they offer me condolences, and skip away. Eventually, it's only me, in my Mexican homespun and no shoes, and Morgan, in his trench coat and his Bill-and-Ted bag. I reach into my shirt and hand him the murder weapon.

"Put it in a plastic baggie first." I say. He nods. "Will, he is...?"

"Taken care of." Morgan grins. "The usual place, November 30, 2013, at 2:57 in the morning. Come if you want."

I shake my head.

"I only need to know that it is done." I say. Morgan claps me on the shoulder, and disappears in a quiet flash.

The fog is slowly waking, sifting by degrees through the shades of grey. I turn the key of my door for the first time, taking care to be quiet. The floor is covered in buttons ripped from a man's shirt, the time on the microwave says 5:50. I don't know if it's right and, suddenly, I don't care. I leave the guns on the office desk, above the stuck drawer, and stuff my homespun in the closet where I used to keep a change of clothes in case I was time traveling. I burn the letter in the fireplace.

I climb up the stairs, and consider showering, but what the hell, we'll need to wash the sheets anyway. I climb into bed, and Rachel turns over, murmuring, and throws her strapping arm over me. I scoot into her, and hold the scar close to my chest. Rachel is warm, and inviting.

And I am never leaving her again.

About R. Jean Mathieu

R. Jean Mathieu is the author of the *No Time* time-active mysteries, as well as short stories ranging from science fiction to fantasy, horror and magical realism. He's been published at MindFlights.com, in *One Weird Idea*, and in the anthology *I, Automaton*. For "The Remedy," he won 3rd place in the 1999 Ray Bradbury Short Story Contest, and for "Gods of War," Honorable Mention for the Cuesta Literary Prize. In 2013, his "The Short, Strange Life of Comrade Lin" won 2nd place in the N3F Contest. He has also been shortlisted in the Writers of the Future contest. You can find more stories and news at rjeanmathieu.com.

Mathieu graduated with his BA in Sociology (with a minor in Business Administration) from Northeastern University in 2014. He presently lives in Guangzhou, China, with two mad people, but expects that situation to change quickly. When he's not writing, studying, brewing, baking, or practicing karate, he enjoys going on rambles and adventures to discover the hidden soul of China. He is awaiting confirmation from the Peace Corps to spend two years in West Africa.

www.ingramcontent.com/pod-product-compliance
Lightning Source LLC
Chambersburg PA
CBHW071234250626
47163CB00001B/181